This faith-based story was great, containing all the elements to keep you reading. It was very well written and it could be a story that anyone of us might go through. I love the scriptures and the history behind the characters with insight on matriarchs. Pat, you definitely know how to tell a story! Great job!

—Melody Vernor-Bartel on *In Defense of Love*

Wow! Oh my! Woweeeee! I absolutely cried throughout this story of two people who found love through the grace of God. Despite Garrett and Shari's doubts about finding love, their faith and trust in God showed them that if they allow Him to order their steps and follow His voice, there is nothing that He will withhold from them. This is a beautiful testimony of the faithfulness of God.

—Jacqueline White on *In Defense of Love*

I love a good underdog story. #teamlandon.

—Mia Harris on *Redeeming Heart*

OTHER CHRISTIAN TITLES BY PAT SIMMONS INCLUDE:

The Guilty series
Book I: *Guilty of Love*
Book II: *Not Guilty of Love*
Book III: *Still Guilty*

The Guilty Parties series
Book I: *The Acquittal*
Book II: *The Confession*

The Jamieson Legacy
Book I: *Guilty by Association*
Book II: *The Guilt Trip*
Book III: *Free from Guilt*

The Carmen Sisters
Book I: *No Easy Catch*
Book II: *In Defense of Love*
Redeeming Heart
Book III: *Driven to Be Loved*

Love at the Crossroads
Book I: *Stopping Traffic*
Book II: *A Baby for Christmas*

Book III: *The Keepsake*
Book IV: *What God Has for Me*

Making Love Work Anthology
Book I: *Love at Work*
Book II: *Words of Love*
Book III: *A Mother's Love*

Single titles
Crowning Glory
Talk to Me
Her Dress (novella)

Holiday titles
Love for the Holidays
(Three Christian novellas)
A Christian Christmas
A Christian Easter
A Christian Father's Day
A Woman After David's Heart (Valentine's Day)
Christmas Greetings

redeeming

Heart

redeeming

Heart

By

PAT SIMMONS

Published by:
Generation Press

ISBN-13: 978-0692434406
ISBN-10: 0692434402

To read more books by this author, please visit www.patsimmons.net.

Printed in the United States of America

Dedicated to the LOST SHEEP
Welcome home.
Luke 15:1–7

Acknowledgements

I praise the Lord Jesus Christ for allowing me to write this story for His glory.

A special shout out to Lisa McKnight of Rhema Services LLC and Angella "AJ" Miller, my good friend, for their insight into the real estate business; and to my cousin, Darlene Simmons, who has had my back since we met through our genealogy research.

I appreciate my husband's patience while I'm in my writing world. I am truly blessed to have Kerry Simmons as a mate for 30 plus years. Thank you, honey!

Many thanks to my late pastor and his wife, Bishop James A. Johnson and Juana Johnson, and to my family and friends who continue to bless me with their support.

A good book is only as good as its editors. Thanks to Chandra Sparks Splond and to EditorNancy from Fiverr.com.

1

What was that?

Octavia Winston's heart constricted as she strained her ears and inhaled. After counting to ten, she exhaled, but she dared not move. As a real estate agent, Octavia was familiar with the mood of a house—its quietness as well as its subtle growing pains. Occupied homes had different vibes from that of a vacant house.

The University City neighborhood was a crossover from St. Louis city to the county. Affectionately called "The Loop" because of its proximity to the elite Washington University, it was known for its thriving nightlife, but in spite of that, this block and adjacent ones had witnessed decades of families come and go. This two-story, three-bedroom brick structure was the latest casualty and now possibly a crime scene. The possible victim: twenty-nine-year-old Octavia Winston.

Lord Jesus, please protect me. Octavia swallowed. She had no escape route in this "lower level"—the preferred term she and her associates liked to use when referring to basements. *Get a grip, girl! Who cares about semantics in a time of danger?*

What was she thinking when she came in for a quick inspection, leaving her phone and purse secure in a locked car while she was trapped in an unsecured house? She scanned the meticulous area for a stick, brick, or any object that actor Macaulay Culkin of the *Home Alone* movies would think of to rig as a weapon. The windows were large enough to peep in or out, but not wide enough for an escape.

Octavia felt trapped as her heart pumped faster. Her skin felt clammy. All she had was her car key, which could gouge out her assailant's eyes. She scrunched up her face at the thought of such a gory scene. Her shoes! Single and living alone, Octavia could fashion a makeshift hammer out of anything. Stilettos had their benefits.

She heard a squeak—time was a wastin'. She had to get past the intruder, out the door and to her car; then she could call the police. "Jesus, I don't know who is upstairs, but please make me a David to whatever Goliath awaits me."

Releasing a deep breath, Octavia gathered momentum like a plane revving up its engines for takeoff. She quietly tiptoed to the base of the steps. Lifting her short skirt even higher, she hiked two steps at a time upstairs toward freedom. As Octavia made it to the landing, she barreled into something—someone—*somebody* who had suddenly appeared out of nowhere. With her adrenaline still charged, she tackled him like a defensive football player. The impact seemed to startle the intruder. *Good.* She took the element of surprise to her advantage.

She scrambled to her feet, but tripped. When her assailant got to his feet, Octavia took off, charging ahead, refusing to look back as she opened the door. Outside, she gulped for air, but kept running. Where were the nosey neighbors when she needed them? She had no witnesses in broad daylight to hear her cries for help.

She scurried across the sidewalk, deactivated her car alarm, jumped into her Taurus and locked the doors. Octavia fumbled with her keys until the right one made contact with the ignition. Steering with one hand, she drove off as she reached for her cell phone on the passenger seat. She used her voice-activation to call the police.

"Nine-one-one. What's your emergency?"

She started rambling, "I'm a real estate agent and…just come quick. It's a big one. He's in the house—"

"Are you still in the house, ma'am?" the female dispatcher queried.

"No. I got away, thank God. I knocked him down, but he kept coming after me—"

"What's the address?"

Octavia could hear the woman pecking on the keyboard as she gave her the information.

"The police are on their way. Stay on the line—"

Too late. Octavia did the opposite and disconnected. She dictated a text to her friend Terri Mack, another agent and broker she worked under: S.O.S. Man in house. Got out. Called 9-1-1.

Pulling over, she took a deep breath to calm her nerves. In the years she had shown houses, this had never happened to her. The city neighborhood was stable with black middle-class homeowners who took pride in their properties. Even though this particular listing was on a nice street, the protocol for all agents was to lock up after each showing. It was her agency's listing, so who had breached security?

She peeked down at her stocking, which had a run in it, and she'd broken a nail from a fresh manicure. Plus, her shoulder was throbbing as a result of the tackle. The fear that held her captive dissipated as defiance surged to the top with a vengeance. Making a sharp U-turn, Octavia raced back to the scene of the crime. Whoever the intruder was, she owed him payback, and watching him get arrested would give her sweet satisfaction.

2

Landon Thomas gritted his teeth and cursed. He had blown his cover. Landon's survival skills as a squanderer were seriously in need of a refresher's course. At six-two, and about two hundred pounds, how could the little fireball who crashed into him temporarily knock the wind out of him?

Granted, he wasn't as buff as he had been since leaving Boston six months ago, but at the least, the woman should have bounced off whatever muscle he had maintained.

Dismissing his wounded pride, Landon had to get out of there. He couldn't risk jail time for various reasons, mainly because he enjoyed freedom. Not only could he not pay for bond, but he wasn't in good graces with anyone who would gladly help him out. He gathered his belongings—the remains of his mass of wealth that he possessed when he began his journey. The prestige and the pampered life he once had back East were gone. It wasn't as if he hadn't put up a fight to hold on to the remnants of his past lifestyle—from creditors and fellow vagabonds.

Life had turned on him with a vengeance, stripping him of almost everything, but Landon refused to lose his dignity, so he clung to his self-pride. Instead of networking with other business professionals, he was schmoozing with homeless associates that were dealt the same fate to survive on the streets of St. Louis.

Nervously, Landon peered through the slits of the wood blinds in the front bedroom, which had been his safe haven. The alternative had been sidewalks, deplorable conditions under overpasses, or shelters as the last resort, so empty houses were like luxury suites at a hotel.

John, Jimmy, Jeremy…J—something from the soup kitchen would chew him out for blowing his cover. His buddy advised him against getting too comfortable in one place and to move on frequently. Landon had overstayed his uninvited welcome by four days. Now, thanks to some good-smelling petite woman, he was about to be evicted from his borrowed residence.

With sirens fast approaching, Landon grabbed his tattered Coach suitcase and slipped out the back door. He cursed at his bad luck that the yard had no bushes and trees for him to hide. He sprinted across the yard and was about to scale the fence when his nightmare came true.

"Freeze! Drop the loot and get on your knees," a man shouted.

What a way to end his life: a gunshot to the back, whether he complied or not. Releasing his suitcase, Landon lifted his arms in the air and turned around. He fell to his knees, hoping the officer's weapon wouldn't accidentally discharge.

"Put your hands up," a short policewoman commanded as she stormed toward him.

"No, put your hands behind your back," a tall male officer contradicted. "And don't move!"

Evidently, they were rookie cops who couldn't make up their minds about how to confine him. "Great," Landon said.

They wrestled with his wrists until they cuffed him, then struggled as they heaved him onto his feet. *Clark* was the name engraved on the male officer's badge as he left Landon's side to retrieve all of his stuff. The other badge read *Jackson*. She was a short African-American woman with a ponytail. Didn't the police academy have a height restriction?

If nothing else, women were drawn to his charm. Landon had mastered the skills of a smooth talker. He had the looks—a stand-in for actor Tyler Lepley, but enhanced and with money—at one time, he had lots of it. He cast a seductive glance at the officer with his hazel eyes, something that would make the heart of anyone with female hormones flutter. "I just wanted shelter," which was true. Landon wasn't a threat to anybody.

"Do you realize you're trespassing," Officer Jackson stated, rather than questioned. "Let's go." She shoved him as a warning that she would use force. He was definitely losing his charm. In his thirty-three years, he'd never had an arrest record, but from the looks of things, one was pending. He had never been homeless either. God wasn't playing fair. Could his life get any worse?

As they came through a wrought-iron gate, another woman— beautiful from a distance—was waiting near the patrol car as they escorted him around to the front of the house. Using her hand to shield her eyes from the sun, she squinted at him.

He gawked at the beauty of her doll-shaped face. The slant of her eyes, either naturally or tricks from makeup, gave her an exotic look. African-American women with any Asian in their blood were his weakness, but who was he kidding? All women were a man's weakness.

She had the most unusual color of light brown hair as if sandy blonde strands were intertwined. The length wasn't important; it was her shiny sassy curls that framed her face that made a man look more than once—he did. As a matter-of-fact, Landon could see himself guiding her soft pointed chin toward his face for a kiss.

In less than thirty seconds, Landon scanned her figure to her attractive toes. Her scandals were a series of straps that tied at her ankles. She wasn't naturally tall, so the heels added height, which drew attention to her well-toned legs, then his eyes traveled back to her face

The softness of her features almost had him groaning until he noticed the lift of a well-defined eyebrow. She looked ticked.

"Landon?" she said in awe, stepping closer. There was that whiff of perfume again, the one that lingered after he was taken down. She was the one who had collided with him. "What were you doing in there?" She pointed to the house.

How did she know his name?

He had a sharp memory, except when it came to women's names and faces after a night's encounter. The next morning, he had forgotten both without regret, but not this woman. They definitely didn't run in the same circles. No man in his right mind would allow her needs not to be met. Landon swallowed.

"I'm visiting," he smarted, stating the obvious. His warped sense of humor was one of his causalities of humiliation.

"Ma'am, you know him?" Officer Clark asked as the unidentified woman eyed him. "Would you like to press charges?"

"No, that's not necessary." His rescuer fanned her hand in the air. "My company owns this property. I just didn't know Landon was here," she said in a manner that made Landon suspicious. "You can release him. I recognize him as one of our patrons at Gateway 180."

Patron at a food pantry was synonymous with homeless. The term took on a whole new meaning when he unceremoniously joined the ranks after losing his senior advertising sales rep position at Foster & Wake Ad Agency in Boston. If she volunteered at the Gateway 180 shelter, then she must have handed him a brown bag lunch a time or two. That was one place Landon didn't want to be recognized. There are always hundreds in the food line, so how come she would remember him?

"He's going with me," she stated, a fist on her curvy hip. She tapped her heel. Judging from her determined expression, she had a scheme brewing.

Not much scared him, but it was something about this soup kitchen volunteer that shook his confidence. "I am?" His jaw dropped.

"Yes, you are." She nodded toward her car.

"You sure, miss?" Officer Clark exchanged a guarded look with his partner who shrugged.

Clearing her throat, Jackson advised, "Then you better lock this place up."

With that said, all eyes were on his unnamed rescuer as she jogged up the stairs and vanished into the house, he guessed to assess any damage for which he might be responsible. The only evidence of his habitation would probably be a ring around the tub after a long, hot bath without the benefits of soap. Landon didn't plan to return to the house tonight without his choice shower gel and toothpaste. He wasn't a thief by trade or hobby, but the idea was tempting.

"Mind if I inspect the contents?" Officer Clark eyed his suitcase.

Landon huffed. He was in no position to demand a warrant. He preferred not to witness the humiliation of someone rummaging through his designer briefs, so he diverted his attention to the brick house. It was a nice starter home for a couple, but the all-white kitchen—cabinets, floor, walls—would definitely need updating if he could afford to buy it, which he couldn't.

Someday, he would get back on his feet—someday, Landon kept reminding himself. Once the officer seemed satisfied with invading his privacy, he snapped the suitcase shut.

As he continued to wait, neighbors stood on their porches to get a preview of what might be on the five o'clock news. Landon was glad to disappoint them. The hottie reappeared and nodded to the police that everything was okay. He cringed after the officer unfastened his handcuffs. He rubbed his wrists, then picked up his tattered suitcase.

Directing him toward her car, the woman got in with such finesse as Landon squeezed his frame into the passenger side for a destination unknown. Adjusting his seat, Landon stretched his legs and refrained from sighing at the feel of her leather seats. When was the last time he had been in a car? He missed the comfort of his silver Corvette, which a loan company had repossessed and another driver was enjoying. Landon had only been four months behind. He was making partial payments with his unemployment checks while he was job hunting. People just didn't cut a guy slack anymore.

I gave you grace, God whispered as if He was tapping him on the shoulder.

He frowned. Grace had not kept him from living on the streets, he thought as his rescuer ordered him to click his seatbelt.

Inserting her Bluetooth in her ear, the woman answered a call and eyed him. "Ah, I'm with Landon," she said as if she was on a covert mission and he was her cargo. "I already did." She disconnected, apparently without any concern about his intentions. They definitely needed to talk about female safety measures when encountering strangers, then he thought about her hit to his gut. She could take care of her own.

Landon frowned. "Two questions."

"Two answers," she said as she pulled into traffic.

"Who are you?"

She laughed, and the sound was melodious. Taking her right hand off the wheel, she extended it for him to shake. "Octavia Winston. Nice to see you again. It's been a while."

How long was a while? Landon frequented three soup kitchens. Gateway 180 offered brown bag lunches seven days a week during business hours. Karen House served cold sandwiches all day and hot lunches Monday, Wednesday and Friday at 12:30. If somehow, he found himself near downtown Clayton, which was upscale, he had until three o'clock to get something to eat at the Bread Company's Care Community Cafe.

Accepting her hand, Landon immediately admired her long fingers and their softness. When he didn't release it right away, she snatched it back. He frowned. "And where are we going, Octavia?"

"Church. I'm glad you don't have a problem with that." She

wasn't giving him an option as she kept her eyes on the road.

Suddenly, Landon felt like gagging on her perfume and bolting from the moving vehicle. "Ah, as a matter of fact, I do." He avoided church whenever possible, even those that sponsored soup kitchens. Church had not been a good fit with his past lifestyle. Landon had been preached to and counseled his entire life. He knew scriptures he didn't want to know and couldn't shake.

When Octavia blasted the radio, Landon was relieved it wasn't gospel music. Coming from a family of musicians, he could play most songs by ear, but he was tired of playing church—inside and outside. Been there and done that. He was free, but destitute.

He eyed Octavia again. Who was this fearless woman who seemed relaxed with a stranger in her car? He could be a felon—or worse, a rapist. "You know, you really shouldn't pick up strangers."

"Yeah. I'm thinking the same thing, too." She tapped a finger on the steering wheel. "But I have mace."

Great. He was being kidnapped by a crazy woman. Now it was time to pray, he thought as he looked out the window from inside the air-conditioned car. It might be hot and humid outside, but at least he had a choice in where he roamed, which was in the opposite direction of a church where he had failed God, himself and four others who needed him.

Octavia regulated her breathing to come off as confident in her actions and not crazy to give a man who she knew nothing about a ride…and to church of all places!

God was definitely working in mysterious ways. As soon as Octavia saw the vagabond's face, he seemed familiar, then his name rolled off her tongue as if she really knew the man. She didn't. That's when God brought the two instances she had seen Landon to mind. Both times, God instructed her to pray for him.

She had without giving much thought to it. Plus, Landon had never exchanged more than a "thank you" with her. Octavia knew his name after overhearing another man say it and she thought it was different.

Do not be afraid. Jesus' voice was soothing and reassuring as the police was about to take Landon into custody. *Take him with you.*

Octavia relaxed at first, but had almost choked on air when the Lord whispered the last part. Once she was in the house to secure the property, she questioned God.

You are serving My purpose. He's My lost sheep. I will perfect the work I began in Landon until the day I return, God said, quoting Philippians 1:6.

And what did that have to do with her? Octavia needed more time for clarification to God's purpose, but she didn't think the officers and Landon would appreciate standing in the hot sun while she had an impromptu prayer meeting, so she had to take God at His Word. Plus, Landon hadn't committed a crime—well, besides breaking and entering.

She wished God had let her in on His plan before she had hysterically texted her broker who rented her office space and who acted like Octavia's mother hen; Octavia's mother had been deceased for years, but Terri Mack was barely six years older than her.

Now, Octavia's feigned calm demeanor had Terri frantic and flustered as she rambled off crime stats. She would deal with her friend later about the perception that all homeless people were unstable.

"I'm harmless," Landon broke into her reverie as if he were picking up on her uncertainty. Maybe the gnawing on her lip gloss was the giveaway.

Believe him, God spoke.

Octavia's amusement was a sham as she put on a brave persona. "And I'm a safe driver. You believe that?" she teased as she jammed on her brakes at a stop sign.

This time, she laughed in earnest. The snapshot of dread on Landon's face was priceless—the payback for him scaring her. He braced his large hands pushed against the dashboard as his tall frame seemed to prepare for impact. It was comical. Octavia was an attentive driver—no tickets to date. Of course she wasn't usually as distracted as she was at the present.

Landon was a minor distraction. She didn't have to stare at his long nose, hazel eyes, and unkempt facial hair to mask the man's handsomeness. His skin seemed so flawless; razor bumps probably had second thoughts about making an appearance. Even his wrinkled clothes made a fashion statement—he looked like a male model on a runway.

Now his scent was another matter. He didn't have a pungent odor, which was saying a lot in this humid weather, but there was definitely a residue of perspiration.

She knew every family, man and woman had a story that had shattered their world and plummeted them into the underground world of homelessness. If it weren't for the grace of God, it could have been her seeking refuge. Despite Landon's current fate, she respected his privacy, but that didn't stop her from wondering about the circumstances that caused his misfortune. "Hungry?"

He frowned. "Never ask a displaced person or a man if he's hungry."

The more he talked, the more Octavia liked his slight dialect and his sense of humor. She nodded. "Good point." When was the last time Landon had a hot meal besides in a soup kitchen? She checked the time and made a detour.

When she pulled into Applebee's parking lot, Landon faced her, merriment dancing in his eyes. "Nice church."

"Don't get too happy. We have exactly an hour and twenty minutes—and don't even think about jumping ship. God always has a tracking device on our whereabouts—physically and spiritually."

"With a beautiful dining companion and a mouth-watering steak—never." Landon hurried out the car as if he was about to stampede the restaurant, but slowed his stride to assist her out the car.

"Thank you." Octavia could never get enough of chivalry. He fell in step with her, but as they got closer to the entrance, his steps quickened, so he could open the door for her.

She might as well take advantage of the treatment as long as she could. She was single with no prospects insight. Like any other woman, Octavia wanted to be loved, wooed and married sooner rather than much later. The holdup was God sending her a Christian man to fulfill the desires of her heart.

3

The *lust of the flesh, the lust of the eyes*....Landon had heard that phrase beat over his head since he was a teenager. He hadn't listened then, but he was trying now to use restraint. Landon exhaled as he tore his eyes away from the view that Octavia was probably oblivious to giving him. She was shapely and had nice legs. Where was the man, husband or significant other that set his woman free like this?

It's the pride of life that keeps you from coming to Me, Jesus said, whispering 1 John 2:16.

Landon grunted as a dispute of God's verdict. He was an outcast. He had nothing—no family, friends, job, food, shelter. His self-worth seemed like all he had left.

Consider the birds in the air. I feed them, I shelter them, I protect them. God whispered Matthew 6:26 to him.

"Hey, are you all right?" Octavia placed a hand on his wrist. Her voice was soft.

He had operated on autopilot, opening the door to the restaurant, but not seeing his surroundings. "Sure," he recovered.

"Don't be nervous about your clothes. I'll ask for a booth up front, okay?" she whispered.

She thought his distraction was about his attire? Her own beauty was the distraction. "Thanks." At the moment, he was hungry and didn't care how he looked.

That wasn't the case a year earlier. Landon had an expensive lifestyle and the money and women to stroke his ego. He always dressed appropriately for any occasion. Landon had been groomed for better than this. It seemed as if every day he was losing a little bit of himself along the way with every sock or shirt that was somehow misplaced.

Yet, Landon was optimistic. He was a survivor, and this too shall pass. He knew his family was praying for him. To them, he was the prodigal son, brother, grandson, cousin and other titles he didn't want to think about. If anyone could get a prayer through, his maternal Miller clan could.

"It's a ten-minute wait," Octavia informed him after speaking with the hostess. "I'm running to the ladies' room. Be right back." She began to strut away before spinning on her heels. "Oh, and don't be a fool and leave without a good hot meal." She lifted her brow, then gave him a point blank expression. "And you don't come across as a fool." She sashayed away.

How quickly she was summing him up, but Octavia had no idea that he called the shots—except when he was hungry.

He took a seat in the lobby across from a couple giving him a curious stare. He ignored them in the same way he had been dismissed many times on the streets when he asked for spare change. It was humiliating and humbling. That had been a sight to see: Landon Thomas begging—a scenario that his estranged family would probably enjoy, recalling the last family gathering where he had been called a fool to his face.

Landon had been summoned to his maternal grandparents' home in Roxbury, a neighborhood of Boston, not far from Dudley Station.

"You're a disgrace to this family. If any child could've been switched at birth, you're the leading candidate," said Moses Miller, the patriarch of the clan. Landon had stared at the older and darker version of himself. His grandfather's hair was no longer gray, but white.

With a calm demeanor and from the comfort of a worn oversized recliner, Moses had rebuked him with such venom that Landon had been caught off guard. He had never seen the seventy-eight-year-old elder so angry as he shook his head. He twisted his mouth as if he was trying to discharge a nasty taste.

No one came to his defense. His parents, aunts, uncles, cousins all seemed to watch with interest. Not one to let anyone see him sweat, Landon was about to take advantage of the pause when his grandfather's tirade continued.

"Landon Thomas, this family—your family—can no longer excuse or support your bad decisions. You were born with a good name, and you're not even thirty-two and you've managed to ruin it!" He pounded his fist on the arm rest. "How many demons are you going to allow to feast off of you?"

"Grandpa, even God said to forgive seven times seventy. I've tried to live right, but the temptation is too great… He knows I'm weaker." Others could pretend they were living holy, if they wanted to, but Landon planned to be true to himself. He stuffed his hands in his designer pants. He was tired of playing church. He knew the scriptures as well as any other family member.

Moses waved his arthritic hand at him. "Enough. *'What shall we say then? Shall we continue in sin that grace may abound? May it never be! We who died in sin, how could we live in it any longer?'* If you don't believe me, pick up your Bible that has your name engraved on the cover. Flip to Romans six…"

There was no need for him to do that. Landon was just exercising his free will. Longevity ran in his family. He had time to serve God, but as Shakespeare said, "To thine own self be true." Landon had done everything in his power not to groan. He made six digits, had a luxury car, condo and money in the bank. All his physical and financial needs were met.

"Grandson, a few days ago God spoke to me. You can't imagine how surprised I was when He revealed to me that you hadn't backslid yet—despite the trail of mess you stirred—but you were in process. That's a warning, Landon. I advise you to take heed."

That meeting had been more than a year ago and since then, God had taken away his livelihood and possessions as a way of punishing him.

"Our table is ready." Octavia reappeared with a smile, so he tucked away the past and allowed her to lead the way.

This time he kept his eyes off Octavia's backside. Sleeping around wasn't on his priority list. As true to her word, the hostess seated them close to the door and handed them a menu.

Landon's stomach growled as he eyed the steak selections longer than he intended. What he wouldn't give for a medium rare sirloin steak, but he wasn't about to take advantage of Octavia's kindness. He forced his eyes about from the images as he closed the menu. Landon sighed, "A burger and fries." Beggars couldn't be choosy, could they? And he definitely was that. He considered himself a social drinker, but he certainly could use a strong drink at the moment. "And a Sprite," he told their server when he arrived at their table.

Octavia was watching him as she closed her menu, too. The way she was staring at him, it was as if she was glimpsing into his soul. "Come on, let's celebrate. Let's do a nine-ounce sirloin with a baked potato and vegetable medley, and two salads," she paused. "Unless you really want a burger and fries...then I guess..."

"I would like that," he said softly as the server revised his order and left them alone again. Over the past months, people's kindness humbled Landon, and so had the begging, but with Octavia, Landon left different. There was more to this chance meeting than he thought. Somehow, Octavia was in tune with him and he didn't know what to do about it.

With loving kindness have I drawn thee. I have loved thee with an everlasting love. God whispered Jeremiah 31:3.

"So, what are we celebrating?"

Octavia dazzled him with a smile as she studied him. "I'll think of something in a minute." She folded her hands. "So Landon, tell me about yourself."

"I'm thirty-three; lost my job when my company downsized. When I couldn't meet my obligations, I decided I needed a change to start over." Landon gave the standard answers and, amazingly, they weren't lies.

"I detect a dialect. New York?"

"Boston."

"Ah." She grinned. "I can see you wanting to relocate to a warmer climate, especially after that season of record snow fall."

"Yep, I was on my way to Texas when I had a series of mishaps..." Landon wasn't about to tell her that he had planned on relocating to Texas or California. With the balance of his savings and cashing out the last chunk of his 401(k) that he hadn't used to pay judgments against him, Landon left Beantown with only three thousand dollars.

A plane ride was out of reach, so he boarded Amtrak, since Greyhound was out of the question—at first. Months earlier, he was on a Greyhound bus and with a lengthy layover in St. Louis, Landon had wandered downtown and stumbled on the building that housed Fleishman Hillard. At one time, the company was the second-ranking public relations company in the United States. It had a stellar record of accomplishments, including producing award-winning commercials for Anheuser-Bush. Plus, the company gave birth to many of the unique advertising blitzes that everyone in the industry wanted to copy.

When Landon returned to the station, he had missed his bus. That mishap hadn't fazed him as he thought about the opportunity to work in his field again. Then reality set in that he was stranded without the bulk of his clothes. The people at Greyhound said they would have it shipped back as soon as they could.

But Landon couldn't wait. He needed a job now. He walked the street until almost dust until he found a shelter. The conditions were awful and smelly, and questionable characters made him sleep with his eyes open. The next morning, he found a cheap motel to shower and iron the few clothes he had, but he needed a shave desperately, so again, he hit the streets until he saw a Walgreens, which commercials boasted were on every corner. They lied. With credit cards maxed and collectors hounding him when he left Boston, he had little cash, which gave him two options.

Hiding his shame, Landon stood outside the store, politely asking for donations for toothpaste, deodorant, and shampoo. Some people had pity and gave him a total of twelve dollars and some change. With the sun becoming unbearable, he went inside to search for clearances. Anything would be a bargain with the little pocket change he had for a watch and electric shaver. Looking around, he eyed the selection. Landon had never been a thief, but he'd never been in desperation mode either. If he was going for an executive job, he needed the toiletries to look and smell the part. He realized there was an art to stealing, and he was an amateur.

Cameras and possibly employees had him under surveillance. "How do they pull this off?" he questioned himself, referring to shoplifters.

"Can I help you, sir?" a young store clerk said, who had suddenly appeared at his side. Landon didn't even notice the short male with Popsicle-red spiked hair. His name tag read *David*.

Landon cleared his voice. "No...well, yes. I've been unemployed for a while. I need a job real soon. Can you recommend some places?"

The young man looked perplexed. "Ah, I'm still in high school. Let me call the manager. He'll know if Walgreens is hiring," he said as if it were a bright idea.

"Wow, I never thought of that. Can I fill out an application?" Landon gave the pretense of feeding into the youth's eagerness.

Grinning, the teenager disappeared. Landon had to make a decision and quick. The Remington Flex 360 Diamond series rotary shaver looked tempting at eighty bucks, but he decided to play it safe with the Phillips Norelco razor that was half the cost. As he tried to quickly stuff it under his shirt, his heart pounded with remorse. Stealing did not give him an adrenaline rush. When he turned around the clerk had returned with a sheet of paper in his hand. The gleam in his eyes was replaced with disappointment. He had been busted after one attempt.

"If I call my store manager, you'll go to jail," David stated as if he were the one scolding a child. Even as Landon towered over him, he felt small.

Removing the razor, Landon handed it over. "Here man."

After accepting the merchandise, David stepper closer. "My church donates food and clothing and other necessities. We'll even come and pick you up for a meal."

"Nah, that's okay." He walked out the store with nothing but the cost of his pride.

Do not worry about your life, what you will eat or drink; or about your body, what you will wear... Is not life more important than food, and the body more important than clothes? And why do you worry about clothes? See how the lilies of the field grow. They do not labor or spin... do not worry, saying, "What shall we eat?" or "What shall we drink?" or "What shall we wear?" I know that you need them, God said, speaking portions of Matthew 6.

Landon ignored Him. *Right,* he thought mockingly. Landon couldn't pray more; he was all prayed out after he lost so much at once—his family's forgiveness, lucrative employment, a spacious condo and a luxury ride.

That had been his first hand at shoplifting. Since that time, he'd swiped small items, all in the name of survival, which he had planned to do later that night for soap and toothpaste before returning to his hiding place that Octavia had discovered.

"Hey," Octavia shook his hand, "you zoned out on me." She

searched his face as if trying to tap into his thoughts.

He cleared his throat and summarized his story with, "In my travels from city to city, I left a trail of clothes as I tried to rid myself of excessive baggage. The end."

What about your spiritual baggage? God asked. *Why are you holding on to that?*

Landon's answer was simple. He didn't know how to let go. People always said they couldn't forgive themselves, so in all honesty, and God knew it, Landon didn't even try. He thought about his worldly possessions. "Suffice it to say, all I have now is that one suitcase." That contained three pairs of pants, six pairs of designer boxers, four T-shirts, and six polo shirts. He knew because he counted them daily.

Resting her dainty chin on her fist, Octavia said, "Uh-oh. This doesn't sound like the old comedy starring Steve Martin and John Candy."

Landon shook his head. "I'm hoping for a happier ending than *Planes, Trains, and Automobiles.*" He shrugged and glanced around the restaurant.

"So you need life's basic necessities."

"For now, but I'm a go–getter. I plan to land with both of my feet on the ground." Despite the odds, Landon never lacked confidence. "What about you? I know you're a real estate agent."

"Yes, and I'm part of the Elite Realtist agents. It's priceless to watch the smiles when someone buys their first home. It's literally a gift from heaven, and I'm so glad to be a part of it."

She captivated Landon when she talked about her passion about what she did. She was enchanting and very beautiful. Despite his hunger, Landon was irked when the server interrupted them with their salads. Seconds later, he was sucked in by Octavia's eloquent grace over their food.

"Lord, we thank You for all things—good and bad—and this meal You have provided. Please bless and sanctify our food and help us to remember those who are hungry, and bless them as You have blessed us. In Jesus' name. Amen."

How many times had he said grace and never thought about others? Even now when there were others in the same boat as him? "Amen."

Octavia didn't say another word as she attacked her food, which was fine with him as he woofed down the juicy steak with as much finesse as possible for a hungry man.

When the conversation did resume, their banter was light hearted—nothing personal, but engaging.

"I should've said it earlier, but I'm sorry for scaring you."

Octavia laughed and patted her chest. "Yes, that was definitely a calling-on-Jesus moment."

The waiter returned and Octavia ordered dessert for them both after he declined, not wanting to drain her of her generosity. Although he wasn't a fan of ice cream, the scoop of vanilla with a chunk of brownie never tasted better. Her eyes sparkled as she watched his gusto.

As he dabbed the corners of his mouth, Octavia asked for the bill. He didn't know which disappointed him more: a woman picking up his tab, going to church or ending the temporary escape she gave him from his present state. But she didn't make him feel like a charity case. Smiling brightened her already gorgeous face as she casually asked, "Do you need a place to stay?"

Landon blinked. He definitely wasn't expecting that. How naïve was she? "Are you offering?"

"I am." She seemed to be smug in her answer. "Who knows? I can be entertaining an angel and may not know it."

Baby, I'm far from an angel, Landon refused to say. "Thank you."

"Not a problem." She stood and gathered her purse. "We still have to stop by my church first."

"Not a problem," he dittoed. So what if he had to brave a few hours in church while she did her thing? It would beat the scolding heat. At least he wasn't about to sit through a Sunday morning sermon. There was no message that God could deliver to him. Landon felt like he had been kicked out of the Garden of Eden. Didn't matter, it was the treat coming after church that he looked forward to.

4

Nothing was going to happen. Octavia knew it; Landon didn't. Smiling, she left him to his musings as she drove off the parking lot. A chime on her phone alerted her to Terri's text.

Rolling her eyes, Octavia ignored it. She had already given her friend/mentor/play big sister/mother hen/crook in the neck an edited version of what happened while she was in the ladies' room.

From the corner of her eye, she saw Landon's head bob and then she heard a light snore. Poor thing. No doubt, he would appreciate a warm bed. In no time, Octavia turned into Jesus the Great Shepherd Church's parking lot. It was bare, except for the janitor and members of the praise team's cars.

She cut the engine and stared at Landon before nudging his shoulder. "We're here. Ready?"

He snapped awake and grumbled, "No. Thanks for asking." He got out first, and with a proud stride came around to her door and assisted her.

His persona was that of an heir to a fortune. Despite the present condition of his clothes, they appeared to be good quality fabrics. The question nagged her again. If God's grace was tangible like clothes and shoes, when and where did Landon fall from it?

"So when was the last time you were in church?"

"A while." Landon shrugged. "I haven't kept track."

That sense of humor again—Octavia was starting to expect it. Landon was easy to be around. She was comfortable. On a first date, she was usually guarded around a man, but this wasn't a date. Still, she liked Landon—as a person, not boyfriend.

In the foyer, the pictures and plaques on the wall seemed to draw in Landon. "Those are from community outreach events," she said, pointing at photographs of children at summer camp, vacation Bible school and an elderly health fair. She steered him inside the sanctuary where the other two praise dancers were talking in front of the pulpit. Landon went no farther than the back row, and he immediately took a seat.

Octavia waved as she approached Kai Kelly and Deb Beavers. The trio rehearsed once a month and danced every other Sunday.

"Who is that?" Kai whispered when she was within hearing distance, peeping over Octavia's shoulder. Men didn't go unnoticed at any church, including hers.

Although their church had an evangelistic and community outreach team that ministered to shelters and families, Octavia wasn't sure how receptive they would be to Landon's plight. She did a speed dial through her mind for an acceptable excuse. "That's Landon. I saw him at one of my properties—" *versus found him,* she thought. "—and we chatted. He's tagging along because we grabbed a bite to eat." She exhaled. "Now, come on, Sister Nosey, let's change so we can practice." She looped her arm through Kai's.

Kai wouldn't budge. "Is he married? Children? Job? What kind of car? And yeah…saved? He looks like a hunk from here."

Octavia shook her head. The two had had conversations in the past about men in the dating pool. Unfortunately, Kai was of the mindset that if the man didn't make more, possess more goods and had a better paying career with a higher education level than her, then he was disqualified from the pool. Octavia always argued,

25

"What about love?" but she never won with her.

Deb squinted at the back of the sanctuary. "He looks kind of suspect to me. Maybe he'll look better in the light."

I wouldn't count on it. "Come on, let's dance." Octavia playfully nudged her. Landon Thomas definitely wouldn't make the cut. In the back dressing room, Kai was like a mouse with a piece of cheese—she wouldn't stop asking about Landon. "Listen, I'll introduce you after practice."

They changed, re-entered the sanctuary and poised at the altar as they waited for the engineer in the sound room to play the first of two of gospel songs by artist LaRue Howard for them to interpret in dance.

Shutting out everything around her, Octavia worked through the routine. If Landon didn't feel the presence of the Lord through this song, then his bones were truly dry. "Lord, let him live again," she whispered, referring to Ezekiel 37.

The sound of congas filtering through the overhead speakers reminded Landon of home. Reared in a musical family, everyone could either sing or play an instrument, many of them both. Only two people in his family played the congas, one being Jamal— Garrett's nephew. The boy could put any adult to shame with his artistic ability. As the music crescendoed, Landon zoomed in on the expression of Octavia's smiling face. It glowed as if God had dusted His anointing on it.

The ladies' movements were as soft and effortless as ballerinas, and hypnotic. It didn't matter that the preacher wasn't on the premises. Landon's spirit was fighting against the praise dancers' overpowering message. He shivered when the artist repeated, "The Majesty is here…"

Without trying, his mind painted the picture of a faceless person sounding a warning alarm to announce the presence of royalty. As the music faded, Landon stopped squirming in his seat. Wiping his self-trimmed mustache, he didn't realize he had broken into a cold sweat. He should get up and wait in the hall for her, but his body wouldn't cooperate.

What am I doing here? He knew better than most that everyone that cried, "Lord, Lord, didn't we do such and such in Your name," wasn't going to heaven. His family made sure every offspring of Moses Miller knew the consequences of Matthew 7:21-23. Although Landon didn't want to go to the first death in hell, he couldn't bring himself to live in a straitjacket, denying himself of the pleasures of the world. Why couldn't he forget all those scriptures?

My yoke is easy! God's voice seemed to walk through the pews toward him.

Landon shivered. "It wasn't for me, Jesus." He bowed his head. Who was more disappointed—him or God? Landon had exercised his free will, and God was wreaking havoc into Landon's life for it.

I've given you relief from the heat while you are living. In hell, there is no relief. God's words were forceful.

Looking up, Landon scanned around the sanctuary. Besides Octavia and her two friends, who weren't paying him any attention, there was no one else in the sanctuary. The skin on Landon's back seemed to sting as if he were shirtless outside in the heat of the day instead of inside the cool air of the church. Then the agonizing sensation lessened.

O taste and see that I am good and My mercy endures forever. Yet, hell exists for sinners who won't repent. God's whisper faded as if He were a breeze passing through.

And there lay his problem. He didn't have it within him to repent—no desire, no conviction and no guilt. Landon was a third-generation Apostolic believer, yet he enjoyed playing the rebellious one against his cousin Garrett whom he had betrayed. Their parents often muttered that their relationship was like Esau and Jacob in Genesis 25. He often wondered if a backslider could truly be redeemed.

Landon needed a distraction from the whole praise dancing that was messing with his head. Sitting back, he stretched his arms across the back of cushioned seats that formed pews. He scrutinized the sanctuary that could easily accommodate a congregation of a couple thousand. A series of track lights were positioned overhead. The podium was of a clear material, simple and functional. A row of chairs for minsters was behind it. Greenery adorned the elevated baptismal pool waiting for converts. Clearly it was the centerpiece of the sanctuary.

When the music stopped and the lights dimmed, Landon thought the show was over. He exhaled.

"Landon," Octavia's voice breathlessly echoed from the stage, "how did we look?"

"Ah." He struggled to his feet and leaned on the back of the chair in front of him. "Perfect." He was ready to get out of there.

Folding her arms, her stance said she didn't believe him.

"I think I was off," the dancer with long braids said matter-of-factly. "Let's go through it one more time."

Of course, Octavia agreed, so Landon gritted his teeth and slid back into his seat. He endured two more practices without them asking his opinion. How long had they been at it? Wasn't the sun setting soon? If his things hadn't been locked in her car, Landon would get out of there and keep walking until he found a hidden cubicle to lay his head for the night.

Suddenly the music stopped. Leaning forward, Landon crossed his fingers and held his breath. Was it over? When the women disappeared from the stage, he exhaled. Countless minutes later, they reemerged. Octavia seemed refreshed from her gospel workout. The other two in the group followed her. He stood.

"Landon, this is Kai," Octavia said, pointing to the woman with the braids, "and this is Deb."

While Deb was the tallest and a looker, her smile was forced. Kai, on the other hand, had a pretty smile, and that was where the attraction stopped. "That's nice of you to sit through our rehearsal.

My husband doesn't have the same patience." Deb paused. "So Landon, what do you do for a living?" She scanned his wrinkled shirt.

"He's in between jobs," Octavia intervened. "If you and Cedric hear of any vacancies, pass it on to me."

"Well, ladies, it's getting late. I'll be happy to escort you to your cars." Landon released his killer smile, but if he didn't get to a free dental clinic soon, he may lose a tooth to a loosened filling.

Kai beamed. "Thank you, Landon." She dragged out his name. "One should never turn down security."

"Or an iron," Deb murmured, but Landon heard it.

An elderly man in work clothes met them as they were leaving the sanctuary. Clearly, Landon's presence had surprised him. "Hello." He frowned, then turned to the ladies. "You sisters truly have the gift of dancing. Let God keep using you. I didn't want to stop the music."

The unseen conductor, Landon surmised.

Thank you, Brother Jeffries," Octavia said, then turned to him. "Ready?" she asked as if inviting a man to stay at her home was a normal occurrence. How could she leave the anointing behind? She was making it easy for him to seduce her, but something about Octavia made Landon want to be a gentleman, protect her and see her smile—all this in less than a day of knowing she existed.

Landon didn't understand it as he escorted Kai and Deb to their vehicles before accompanying Octavia to hers. Once she was behind the wheel and strapped in, Octavia paused before starting the ignition. Landon wondered if she was having second thoughts about inviting him into her home.

He braced for Octavia to rescind her offer as he glanced out the window. It was probably for the best. She didn't. Instead of playing the radio, she opted to hum the song she'd danced to numerous times. No doubt, he would hear music in his sleep, but who cared. He would be in a soft bed.

About thirty minutes later, Octavia drove into a neighborhood with overbearing trees. The bright street lights cast shadows against them. The block was a mixture of strategically placed apartment buildings between every couple houses. It worked in the overall landscape.

Parking in a driveway, she turned off the ignition and faced him. "Okay, we're here. Get your things."

This woman was too easy, too trusting and too beautiful. The temptation was too ripe. "I appreciate this, Octavia, but I hope you don't pick up strays—" he didn't like the sound of that—"I mean, don't do this all the time," Landon felt obligated to mildly scold her as if she was one of his two sisters, although he might be talking himself out of a soft mattress.

"I'll never tell. Besides, what you consider as strays, in Luke 15, God calls lost sheep."

Right, being led away for the slaughter. Can we forget the Scriptures? Landon clenched his teeth to keep from asking. After getting his suitcase, he turned around and scrutinized the building. As a real estate agent, he would have expected her to live in a classy house or pricey condo. Landon cleared his throat. Beggars couldn't be choosy. "Hey, nice place."

"Glad you like it." Together, they walked the short path. Stopping at the door, she pressed the bell.

He frowned. Where were her door keys? Landon didn't consider she might have a roommate. An older gentleman opened the door. She had said her father and step-mother relocated to Florida, so who was this guy? Landon squinted. The man didn't look that old, even with his receding hairline and round stomach.

"Octavia, you're later than you said—had me a little worried." He scratched his head.

"Sorry, Brother McCoy. You know how I get carried away with rehearsal."

Landon snickered.

Octavia cut her eyes at him before making the introductions.

"This is Landon. He's the one who needs a place to stay and the works."

Why was he relieved and disappointed at the same time with her sleeping arrangements? "The works?" Landon repeated.

Brother McCoy smiled and extended his hand to Landon. "Yes. An assessment of your job skills and toiletries, underwear..." he continued talking as he led them inside.

Landon was well aware of the routine shelter evaluation upon entry. Landon had gone through the motions before at other places to update his résumé, but what was the sense of printing them out? He needed clean professional clothes, preferably dry cleaned, a rental car with a GPS and a list of companies hiring upper management. If he couldn't earn the six-figure salary he once enjoyed, he could manage with seventy thousand minimum. Who was he kidding? At the present, he would be happy with a map and a bicycle.

With the last one hundred dollars in his pocket, he was running out of options. Half of it had come from a stranger who reminded him of his grandfather. Along with the money, the man gave him a business-size card with no name, no number, just a prayer printed on it. Landon had actually prayed that day with tears in his eyes, thanking God for the handout.

Although Landon needed steady income, he would probably be working for free. Of all the things he learned from his family, financial responsibility stuck. If he created a debt, he believed in paying it. Shamefully, he had filed bankruptcy, but some judgements the court wouldn't dismiss and honestly, Landon wanted to be held accountable. What a mess he had made of his life. No doubt, garnishments would attack his first paycheck like locusts in a wheat field. With the way his luck was going, he might remain in poverty for decades to come.

"Thank you, Brother McCoy, for finding space with short notice," Octavia said and turned to Landon.

She took his hand and squeezed it. Hers was soft. Octavia's lips parted as if she was about to say something, then changed her mind. Instead, she nodded, then headed for the door.

Landon frowned at Brother McCoy. "Give me a sec." Still holding onto his suitcase, he hurried out the door and caught up with Octavia before she got in. "You know, I thought you were taking me to your house."

Her smirk turned into a harmonious laugh. She winked. "I bet you did. You're welcome." She got in and drove away.

Staring at her fading taillights, Landon shook his head. "She played me."

5

Back inside the shelter, Brother McCoy was standing in the same spot Landon had left him.

"Ready for your tour now?" His eyes danced with mischief as if he had been in on the joke with Octavia.

Landon nodded and proceeded to follow him throughout the two-story facility. He guessed the director's age to be somewhere near fifty years old. His mannerisms reminded him of his eighty-year-old grandfather. Not many men possessed the combination of an air of authority while being seemingly approachable.

He and his grandfather, his father, mother...and so many others had separated on bad terms long before he had made the decision to leave town and start over. It was draining rehashing his past as he contemplated his future. *This is just a temporary bridge to cross,* he reminded himself.

I died on a cross for you, God whispered.

Why did God have to constantly tap into his thoughts? *I know,* he silently admitted as he kept in step with Brother McCoy. The facility looked more like a residence than the compound that had been a shelter he had he lodged in overnight. The floors and walls were clean and the place smelled of disinfectant.

Turning down a short hall, Brother McCoy invited him into a small but well-organized office. Once they were seated, the formalities got underway with the customary intake of information, which outlined the do's and dont's for residents at the shelter. Despite his estranged relationship with his parents and two sisters, he always gave his mother's name and number for contact in the event of an emergency, basically his demise.

"Breakfast will be served from seven to eight-thirty. You're expected to be out searching for work by nine, except on the weekends. That's your free time. Dinner will be served at six-thirty….residents can stay here for up to ninety days. If you need additional time, you can discuss it with your case worker who will be assigned to you."

Landon nodded. "Thank you for your generosity. I hope not to be here that long. I've got to keep moving—"

"I don't know where you came from or what circumstances caused the state you're in," Brother McCoy seemed to study him, "but you first have to reconcile the past so that God can restore anything you've lost. Restoration comes after repentance. Ask God for it."

Maybe, it was exhaustion or irritation, but Landon had heard enough about God for one day. He became indignant. "What makes you think I haven't?"

He shrugged. "I say this to all the men who come through those doors. Second, third, and fourth chances aren't a given. Only when you fix whatever was broken in the past can you move on, or else you might slip back in the same circumstances. Take it personal if it applies."

"Sorry." Landon rubbed his head. He had jumped to conclusions. "Long day. My past is the past. Sometimes, instead of patching a favorite shirt, you have to replace it with a new, better one."

"Ahh." Brother McCoy grinned and nodded. "A man with wisdom, and if he lacks any, let him ask of God who gives it liberally without making the asker ashamed. That's James 1:5."

He was starting to sound like his grandfather. Landon feigned a yawn, hoping Brother McCoy would take the hint. The only thing he wanted was a shower and a bed free of lice and bed bugs. Maybe, they could bump heads in the morning. "I really do appreciate you allowing me to stay here, and I will abide by your rules."

Closing his file, Brother McCoy stood. "Then we'll get along fine. Come on, I'm sure you are tired." Landon grabbed his suitcase and followed him up a narrow passageway. They were almost at the end of the hall when Brother McCoy tapped lightly on the door before inserting a key to open it. "You're on the second floor and share a room with Grady Bacon."

With a name like Grady, Landon wasn't expecting to see a man under sixty, but his roommate appeared to be barely a teenager outfitted in a dingy muscle man T-shirt. He hadn't made a move to answer the knock. Glancing up from his cell phone, Grady acknowledged him with a nod. Brother McCoy made quick introductions, then left.

Landon rested his suitcase on the twin bed that resembled a cot, but higher, then sat himself.

"So, what you in for?"

"Excuse me?" Landon was not interested in a meet and greet.

"Did you get put out...?" Grady rambled off possible scenarios.

With his elbows on his knees and his shoulders slumped, Landon half-heartedly answered, "All of the above."

Grady reached over and offered him a fist. Landon obliged to bump it with his. He didn't want to be in close quarters in a hostile environment. Without asking, Grady told more about himself than Landon cared to know: Twenty-one, just got his GED, three children and recently unemployed. "Mac's been good to me. He got me on at Wal-Mart. I don't want to be locked up for two years because I didn't pay child support. It's only a misdemeanor."

"No, a Class C Felony," Landon corrected.

"Whatever. I'm cool. It's minimum wage, but I've got to start somewhere." He flexed his muscles.

Somewhere, Landon mused. Where was his somewhere with a BA from Boston University, an MBA from Emerson College and seven years as a PR account executive. Despite his résumé, he was in the same boat as Grady—displaced. Landon shared a little—very little—about himself. The young man seemed to be intrigued by Landon's short version of his riches-to-rags story. "Well, I'd better head to the showers."

"All right." Grady nodded as he reached for a green pocket Bible.

Oh no. *As long as you don't talk about Jesus, we'll get along,* Landon thought as he walked out the room with the goody bag from Brother McCoy with a bar of Zest soap.

6

"**W**hat a day." Octavia exhaled as she waited for a red light to change. *Why do I feel like I dropped off a stray pet at an animal shelter?*

He needed rescuing, the Lord answered her.

She wished Jesus would have let her in on His plan before Landon scared her half to death. After God told her not to be afraid and she finally relaxed, Octavia enjoyed Landon's company.

She smiled. If he was shaved and cleaned up, Landon would be handsome she supposed. It wasn't the striking color of his eyes that caught her attention—it was the depth of turmoil that filled them, but with one blink, she erased the haunting from her sight.

Octavia admired Landon for not having a blame-other-people attitude about himself. Despite his plight, he possessed confidence when he spoke and walked, yet the moment he stepped inside church, his demeanor changed drastically. Clearly, he didn't want to be there.

Landon continued to invade her thoughts until Terri's ring tone played on her phone. Taking a deep breath, she tapped her ear piece and prepared for a tongue lashing. "Hey, girl."

"This is not a 'hey girl' moment," Terri warned. "It's an 'are you out of your mind?' followed by 'are you okay?' moment after that stunt you pulled today. Please tell me that homeless guy didn't hold you at gunpoint—or rather fork point since you fed him." Terri didn't give Octavia space to explain, ranting on and on. "And let me go on record and say, you've lost your mind!"

Yeah, well, Octavia thought so too—at first. She could have been raped as some female real estate agents had been in the past because the listing agent didn't make sure the house was secured. It had truly been a "but God" moment. She lifted one hand in silent praise before turning into the driveway of her beige brick ranch house. The stone-covered double pillars and the arch entryway created a stately welcome home after a long day. The foreclosure home had been a good investment.

As Octavia parked in her garage, Terri gasped for air. She smirked, hoping her friend used her inhaler before she upset herself. "Listen, granted I was afraid..." She paused.

Despite how many testimonies she had shared with Terri, her friend couldn't believe God would waste His time talking to ordinary people like them. Terri labeled herself a Christian as if it were a multiple-choice answer on a quiz. Her faith walk was questionable. That was reason enough for Octavia to hold her tongue about what God had told her about Landon. Lowering her garage door, Octavia got her things and crossed the threshold into the kitchen. She deactivated her home security alarm, then rested her keys and purse on the counter. "He was harmless. Plus, the police were going to arrest him."

"And you stopped them? He probably would have appreciated a bed and three meals a day!" Terri raised her voice. "Besides, that's police protocol for someone who breaks and enters into a property without their name on the deed."

Octavia rubbed her feet as she kicked off her shoes before making her way to her bedroom. The only thing she wanted was a cool shower to wash away the perspiration from the day's humidity. "I'm fine, really,' she tried to reassure her so they could end the call.

"Hmm, well, the next time you send me an S.O.S. text that someone is in one of our unoccupied properties, you'd better let the police do their job! Then when I call back, you're calm and casually give me some man's name whom I've never heard you mention before—I can count your male friends on one hand—riding shotgun in your car. Of course, if you let Andre and me introduce you to some of his friends…"

Not this same argument again? Octavia groaned. Whether they were in a Wendy's drive-thru line or shopping for pantyhose in Target, Terri would bring up her matchmaking services. "What does another man have to do with any of this?" Her friend's reasoning never made sense, so why did Octavia even bait her? "Thanks, Terri. I appreciate you and your hubby looking out for me. God knows who I need in my life and He knows what type of man I want. The Lord is my matchmaker."

Terri huffed. "Right. Now, back to the Mr. Wrong you let in your car today; it's a good thing you didn't offer him room and board. Tavie, sometimes, I think you're too generous."

"I did."

"You what?" Terri shrieked in her ear. "Your mind is gone. Are you sure he didn't hit you over the head with an empty beer bottle or something?"

Fits of laughter exploded from Octavia's lips until tears streaked her cheeks. "Girl, Landon is at Mac's Place, not mine—you know Brother McCoy's mission shelter to help men get back on their feet."

Terri didn't muffle her sigh of relief. "You had me going. Now I can enjoy my dinner, but this conversation isn't over. At least he doesn't know where you live."

"Girl, I forgot to tell you—"

"Don't even say it, Octavia. You may have acted crazy today but I know you ain't stupid. Bye," Terri ended their call.

Once Octavia had showered and slipped into something comfortable, she grabbed the phone to call her younger sister,

Olivia, who was attending law school in DC. She wanted to get her take on the day's events. Octavia wasn't surprised, but definitely disappointed when she got Olivia's voice mail. "Call me when you get a chance—it's not an emergency," she said, then disconnected.

Five years younger, Olivia shared the same mannerisms as Octavia. They were the same height with the same light brown skin. Only Octavia inherited the blondish-brown hair that easily identified her. Olivia's hair was jet black like their father's and longer.

Octavia smirked when she thought about Landon again. She might not have a crisis to tell her sister about, but today was definitely not the norm in her life as a realtor. The first thing Olivia would want to know is if Landon was cute. "Definitely!" She blushed for noticing.

7

Saturday morning at Mac's Place, Grady took the honor of introducing Landon to the thirty-plus other men during breakfast. Their ages and ethnicities varied, so did their demeanor. Some appeared content in their plights; others seemed to resent it. Landon guessed he was somewhere in the middle.

As a combined effort after each meal, the men were expected to sweep the floors, wipe off the tables and perform other household chores to earn their keep. When the kitchen was restored, his options were watching a program on the community television voted by a majority, stepping outside for a smoke or taking part in a card game.

Spying the pair of community computers in the corner, Landon headed in that direction. Until yesterday, he had been in a hurry to get to Texas—Houston, Dallas, Austin, it didn't matter, as long as it was far away from home. That was before Octavia knocked him to his knees—literally.

He logged onto the computer and began job searches in St. Louis, thinking about Octavia. She was sincere, sassy and witty. Landon chuckled. She purposely planted a seed in his mind that she was inviting him to her house. The joke had been on him. He grunted, then refocused on getting gainfully employed.

"You look deep in thought," a deep voice said over his shoulder.

Landon stiffened. How could someone sneak up on him like that without him sensing their presence? Since he had been in "transition," Landon tried to stay in tune with his surroundings and possessions. He may have been called a "pretty boy" growing up, but looks were deceiving. He knew how to defend himself whether with a fist, kick or weapon. Certain neighborhoods in Boston dictated that.

Turning around to face the intruder, Landon blinked. An unrecognizable man towered over him. At first glance, his dark skin reminded Landon of his cousin from back home, which made him do a double take. Unlike Garrett's, there weren't any darts shooting from his eyes. All Landon saw was kindness.

This stranger with close-cropped hair and a clean-shaven face was dressed in a high-end polo shirt and slacks. He wore an intangible air of confidence. Landon tried not to stare at the man's shoes which would only remind him of the dozens he had lost because he couldn't pay rent on the storage unit.

Landon got to his feet to match the man's height, only to be a couple of inches shorter at six-two. As his nostrils flared, Landon unsuspectedly inhaled the man's cologne. That was another thing he had to forfeit—his designer colognes. Whoever this interloper was, somehow he didn't fit the MO of the other residents there—his eyes were full of life.

"I didn't mean to startle you." He gave him a ready smile and stuck out his hand. "Rossi Tolliver."

He gripped it. "Landon Thomas."

Grinning, Rossi peered at the computer screen, invading what little privacy Landon had.

That gesture put Landon on the defensive. Although he hadn't slept with a woman in more than a year—sixteen months, if he was counting—he wasn't desperate to visit porn sites, if that's what

Rossi was trying to verify and Landon was about to tell him that, too.

"I recognized that company's logo," Rossi explained. "So you're looking for a sales position?"

"Senior advertising rep," he emphasized *senior*, not entry level. He needed to make a lot of money—some financial obligations he couldn't let go of.

Rossi nodded, grabbed a chair nearby and made himself comfortable. "Do you need any help updating your résumé?"

Who was Rossi Tolliver? Landon took his seat again. "Résumés don't land jobs; people skills and networking open doors."

"Sounds like you've had a lot of doors shut on you lately."

The man had no idea, but Landon was a private person. What little he had shared with Octavia the day before was more than he had divulged with anyone since he had been on the road. Landon squinted. "Are you my caseworker?"

"Oh no, Mac and I are friends, and I drop by from time to time. He thought I should introduce myself to you." Before Landon could ask why, Rossi continued, "Do you have any plans for Sunday?"

Folding his arms, Landon grunted and gave him a pointed look. "Not for church."

"I see." Rossi scratched his jaw. "Since you're searching for employment, there's a networking event tomorrow afternoon at the Sheraton Hotel. I think you should attend."

An opportunity. Landon's heart leaped with hope, then reality set in. "Thanks, but I can't go looking like this," he said as Rossi scanned his attire and asked his shirt, pants and shoe size. "I may not have much left, but I've been able to hold on to one shirt and slacks, and my dress shoes…" They definitely needed a good hand polish. He fingered his curls. His appearance also needed enhancing.

"I tell you what, why don't you tag along with me to my

barber? I'm sure he could fit you in. Bring your clothes. There's a one-hour cleaners nearby."

Swallowing, Landon's heart soared again. Suddenly, he had a good feeling about things turning around. Landon grinned and shook Rossi's hand. "Deal."

Rossi stood. "Let's do it, bro."

8

Octavia sold the house on Corbitt to a young couple as a starter house. When she walked in this morning, she couldn't help but be reminded of Landon's presence. He also reminded her of a valuable lesson: never go into a property without her cell phone and a can of Mace, even if it was supposed to be secure. Well, the Mace was her idea. She was tempted to call Brother McCoy to check up on him—no—she actually wanted to see him, but she would wait a couple of days. Even though she enjoyed his company and was rooting for him to get back on his feet, Octavia didn't want to come across as if she was chasing behind him.

She had to get her mind off the man, which invaded her thoughts off and on for most of the day. She text Terri the good news and within minutes, her friend called with congrats. They chatted a few minutes before Terri said her goodbye, so she and her husband could enjoy their movie night.

Having her fill of movies and books, Octavia tried Olivia again. Voice mail. Knowing her sister on a Saturday night, she was probably hanging out with one or more of her sorority sisters who attended the same church.

When Octavia attended Xavier University in Cincinnati, Ohio, she hadn't thought about pledging a sorority. Besides studying, Octavia had been active with the church's youth ministries. Fast forward ten years, what happened to those friendships? She really craved the bond of a girlfriend sisterhood. Maybe it was her loneliness talking again.

How did Landon handle the loneliness? She couldn't imagine being homeless, yet she admired his upbeat attitude. Didn't he have family and friends who cared about what happened to him?

To fill her boredom before bedtime, she was about to watch a home decorating show when her father called. She smiled. Thank God for family. "Hi, Daddy."

"How's my favorite daughter?" Octavia laughed at his standard greeting. Melvin Winston said the same thing to Olivia. "Have you sold any million dollar mansions this week?"

"Not yet."

"Well, it's coming. God is faithful." Her father brought her up to date with what was going on in his retirement community, with her step-mother—who was sweet, but a quiet woman; the opposite of her mother whose gregarious personality was contagious—and his concern about his daughters' finding happiness. "I think I should be a grandpa."

"I think you should keep praying that God will send you a godly son-in-law—" she teased.

"Who will love and treat my favorite daughter as a princess," he stated.

That was the extent of their conversation about her lack of viable candidates. She spoke briefly to her step-mother, then they signed off until next time.

The next morning, Octavia woke hyped. She always was when her praise team would perform before morning service. She prayed, showered and ate. When it came to dressing, Octavia stared at her hair in the mirror.

The bouncing curls she had days ago were limp and wouldn't hold up on another hot summer day. She quickly brushed her hair up into what she called a ballerina's ball on top of her head. She applied light makeup only because of the mixer with other agents, loan officers, banks and mortgage companies she was attending after service. Otherwise, she wore very little makeup in the summer.

Her A-line dress was simple in style; its white color gave it elegance. Next, Octavia slipped into her heels with the double straps at her ankles that complemented the twin ones across her toes. All this fuss for attire she would have to change once she got to church. She chuckled.

Grabbing her purse, lightweight shawl and Bible, Octavia headed out the door. As she hummed to her favorite gospel songs while she drove, she thought about her recent praise dance rehearsal, which made her think about Landon again.

She arrived at church and welcomed the hugs and greetings of "Praise the Lord" as she quickly hurried to the women's lounge to change into her praise uniform.

"Hey, Tavie. Have you seen Landon?" Kai dragged out his name, then capped it with a smile.

"I haven't, but when I see him, I'll tell him you asked about him."

That seemed to make Kai's day as she beamed. "Do that."

Deb shoved her. "Girl, please. Find a man who will at least iron his shirt."

"Sisters, please," Octavia jumped in. "As Pastor Willis would say, 'Let's focus on Christ.'"

To be a part of any auxiliary at Jesus the Shepherd Church, the pastor required members to represent Christ completely in soul and spirit, and come to Him with a clean heart when performing a service or sit out. He didn't tolerate foolishness when it came to God.

"You're right," the two agreed with Octavia, then Deb led them in prayer before they joined the praise singers in the sanctuary. "Lord, in the mighty name of Jesus, forgive us of thoughts and deeds that don't reflect You and sanctify our minds to draw lost sheep to the Shepherd in Your holy name, Jesus."

They mumbled their amens. They entered the auditorium, swaying to the music. "His Majesty Is Here" was her favorite song as she imagined King David dancing before the Lord and the twenty-four elders bowing down and worshiping the Lamb as described in the Book of Revelation.

Octavia inhaled the words when the song alerted the congregation that the Majesty was in their presence. By the time it ended, she was always blurry eyed and in awe. Back in the changing room, she composed herself and slipped back into her dress.

Deb joined her husband while Octavia and Kai sat together whenever they praise danced. Pastor Willis made his way to the podium to welcome guests and make a few announcements before opening his Bible. "Let's turn to Matthew 25." He paused while the congregation complied. "We've all heard the parable about the ten virgins who knew the groom was coming but still weren't ready. Don't let that happen on your watch. Whether you know or don't believe, Jesus is coming back. Consider this your public service announcement. Be prepared with the Holy Ghost, which is the oil mentioned in Matthew...." As he preached, there was a hush throughout the sanctuary.

"The Lord is sending out warning signs. Is your soul ready? We talk about being prepared for disasters, but what about the great disaster that will destroy both body and soul mentioned in Luke 12:5. God is soon to come in the blink of an eye, or before our next breath."

As Pastor Willis pleaded for souls to repent, Octavia didn't know when the sermon ended and the altar call began, but she closed her Bible as dozens walked down the aisle for prayer, baptism or to seek the Holy Ghost. This portion of the service was always festive with celebration and high energy, and Octavia never wanted it to end, but she had another engagement, so after the offering and benediction, she and Kai hugged and said their goodbyes.

She waved at Deb and her husband, Cedric, as she crossed the parking lot. Her stomach growled as she slid behind the wheel of her car and blasted the air. There would be light refreshments at the upscale mixer that was by invitation only for Million Dollar Club real estate agents and their guests. There weren't many African-American agents in attendance—sometimes by choice, other times by exclusion.

Every year, Octavia always came up short in home sales to make the achievement, but Terri, who had made the Million Dollar Club countless times, tried to keep her in the loop about these functions, which were pivotal in reaching that goal.

Twenty minutes later, she checked her appearance in the mirror and refreshed her lip gloss. Her ball was still intact after her dance routine and the wrinkles to her simple white dress were minimal. Taking a deep breath, she said a quick prayer that God would open doors to get more business. Before the year was out, she wanted to make the Million Dollar Club. So far her house sales barely reached four hundred thousand dollars. "But God, You are faithful!"

She stepped out with her purse filled with a stack of business cards, then reached back for her shawl. Carter Mortgage, housed in a historic building, was owned by generations of the elite Carter family. Once she graced the entrance, Octavia admired the architecture, which could serve as a backdrop for a wedding photographer with its sculptured high ceilings and marble floors.

The furniture in the lobby had been rearranged since the last time she had been there. Counter tables were sprinkled throughout for people to stand, sip and chat, as well as sectional seating for cozy conversations.

A server greeted her and offered her a glass of champagne. She declined, eying a buffet spread in view. Surely, there would be bottles of water to quench her thirst.

As she inched her way toward the food, she slipped out a few business cards to have handy in case she was stopped before she reached the table. She had yet to see Terri or a familiar face. A gentleman stepped in her path and grinned.

"Well, hello there." He scanned her attire and lingered at body parts that made Octavia uncomfortable. She schooled her disgust with a sweet smile. "Hi. I'm Octavia Winston."

"I'm Frank Lindell…"

Who didn't know the Lindell name in St. Louis? He was responsible for most of the new developments near Lambert Airport and beyond. "You construct the most beautiful homes," she complimented.

When he held his hand out for a shake, she placed her card between his fingers. She was interested in business and nothing else. Something told her she would have to pry her hands from his grip.

Octavia guessed he was in his mid-forties. She was sure his blue eyes were his best asset when it came to attracting a woman, but she wasn't one of them.

Clearly, the man didn't want to talk business, so she discreetly inched her way to table. "I apologize. I just came from church and I'm a bit hungry."

He nodded and waited patiently as she placed hors d'oeuvres on her crystal luncheon plate.

"Let's chat a bit," he suggested as he led her to a counter table a group had just vacated.

Again, he waited as she blessed her food, then began to nibble. Surprisingly, Frank talked about another phase of his existing development. Maybe she had misjudged him.

"I would like to discuss more of my vision over dinner and escort you to some other events—introduce you to colleagues and associates."

Dinner? Octavia knew how to separate business from pleasure. "I would appreciate that. Since my broker invited me here today, I would love to return the favor and bring her along." She didn't realize she had eaten everything on her plate until a server reached for it and she consented. After dabbed her mouth, Octavia extended her hand for a shake—briefly, then she excused herself.

Octavia exhaled. While looking for Terri, she introduced herself to other professional women until she saw a familiar face and made a beeline in his direction.

"Minister Tolliver, it's good to see you!" Octavia smiled and gave him a loose Christian sisterly hug. She didn't have any brothers, but Rossi was a good stand-in. "What are you doing here?"

"Same as you." He laughed. "Rubbing shoulders with moneymakers to let them know that downtown East St. Louis had a face-lift and is open for business."

Rossi had given the depressed business district in the Metro East more than a face-lift. Her friend and his cousin had designed and constructed a business/loft/shopping area that they named Tolliver Town. Octavia had worked with him in getting small businesses, such as classy boutique shops and restaurants, to lease spaces. With incentives like low rent for one year and other perks, spaces were filled within months. It had been a win-win for all. Now the Tolliver cousins were on to phase two.

Realizing her rudeness, Octavia turned to apologize to the other man, then blinked. Her mouth opened, but the words were delayed. "Lan–Land...my Landon? Wow." She scanned him from head to toe. "You cleaned up." She blushed.

"Your Landon." Landon snickered. "I like that. Does that mean I get a hug, too?"

"No," she teased and smacked his hand. She hadn't meant to call him *her* Landon, as if he belonged to her. He wasn't a stray dog she found—he belonged to God. To keep from staring, she faced Rossi again. "I see you met Minister Tolliver."

Landon seemed surprised and not too pleased by the revelation. "I didn't know he was a minister."

Rossi slipped his hands in his pockets and rocked on his heels, then shrugged. "It's a title. We all have them."

The man was as humble as pie, handsome and successful—a good combination for husband material, and every woman seemed to be after her "big brother," but Octavia knew his heart belonged to one woman and Rossi had yet to tell her. "So how do you two know each other?"

"I had no idea when I stopped by Mac's Place that Landon had met my favorite sister." Rossi chuckled. "Karyn and her staff treated him to the works at Crowning Glory, so that he could network today. Now, I see God was watering a seed you had planted." He winked.

Well, Jesus, You sent the right man to rescue Landon. He was definitely in good hands with Rossi. She guessed her assignment with Landon was finished, except to stay prayerful. If Octavia could read Rossi's mind, he was probably thinking like her that God had Landon on some type of course, and she and Rossi were being used as relay runners to get Landon to the next destination.

"I know that Scripture," Landon said as if in a warning tone.

That was a good sign. She was attracted to men who liked to read and one who read his Bible got her attention. Before Octavia could engage him more, Terri was in her peripheral vision, waving frantically at her. "I better go mingle if I want to roll with the big dogs this year. Minister Rossi, I'll see you at the tent meeting next weekend?"

"I look forward to being there," Rossi nodded.

Octavia chanced another glance at Landon. Wow. Clothes may not make the man, but clean and pressed garments uncovered the hunk before her. Plus, he read his Bible! Her heart danced. Enough ogling, she chided herself as she met Terri halfway.

"Girl, where have you been? I've been looking for you," Terri scolded in a hushed tone. "There are some contacts I want you to meet." She glanced over her shoulder. "Who were you talking to?"

Peeping over her shoulder, Octavia was surprised to see

Landon and Rossi watching her. When Rossi waved, Terri, recognizing him, waved back.

"Who's that other good-looking guy?" Terri asked, elbowing her.

"Landon."

"Who?"

"The guy that was in the house," Octavia reminded her.

Terri seemed to gasp for air. "You're kidding me." She squinted, then grabbed Octavia's hand and tugged her in another direction. "We'll talk about your charity case later. Right now, I want to introduce you to some new circles of CEOs, attorneys…"

9

A minister, huh? Landon thought the kindred connection with Rossi was because…Landon didn't know why. Landon didn't know what disappointed him more—Rossi's status or Octavia not acknowledging him. Rejection empowered him to come back swinging with a vengeance, but something told him not to tangle with Octavia because he would lose, and he wasn't referring to his meager possessions, but his heart.

He had never seen a woman of color with that blondish shade of brown hair. It had to be natural because it blended with her skin tone, which made her stunning with little effort. Although the curls she wore the other day came off as sassy, today with her hair swept up in a ball, she looked like a princess. Beautiful didn't begin to describe her. While she had been chatting with Rossi, Landon admired her shapely figure in that white dress. It might have been hot outside, but one look at Octavia and he was refreshed.

When she strutted away, she seemed to glide across the room, and she didn't go unnoticed by others who parted a path when they saw her coming. As Octavia disappeared into the crowd, Landon remembered to breathe. That woman had his heart pumping as if he was running on a treadmill. "Wow." Drawing his eyes away, he squinted at Rossi. "So did you two ever have a thing going?"

"No," Rossi answered easily. "We're brother and sister in Christ. Listen, I don't know your story, but I know the look and I know her story. Don't mess with Octavia unless you're planning to put Christ first in your life."

And that was a problem. People thought repenting was easy, but it was more than saying, sorry. He should know as one who had never allowed Jesus to be a barrier from him getting whatever or whomever he wanted in the past, and he had lost playing those games. "Noted. So why didn't you tell me you were a minister?" As a server walked by, Landon eyed the flute of champagne. He needed something stronger.

"You didn't ask me," Rossi stated, pulling him back to the conversation. "Is that supposed to change our friendship?" He crossed his arms in a challenge, throwing the ball into Landon's court.

Rossi was right—he hadn't asked. Landon hadn't asked Rossi or Octavia for anything. Yet the two had freely given to him. *Plus, who am I kidding?* Little by little, Rossi made him feel like Landon Jeffery Thomas instead of a nameless, faceless person on the street. He owed Rossi, and he wasn't talking about the cost for the spa treatment he had received the day before at his family's barber/beauty salon. Rossi had his clothes pressed and his shoes shined. Rossi had made introductions nonstop since they arrived and he talked about Landon as if he had known him since birth.

If only the man knew the laundry list of sins Landon carried and couldn't dispose of. Still, he needed a friend—someone like Rossi who didn't make him feel like a charity case, but Landon wouldn't be a man if he didn't hold on to some pride. "As long as you don't hound me about going to church, I would like that." Landon didn't crack a smile. He was serious.

"Works for me." Rossi extended his hand. "C'mon. Let's mingle and get you back on track."

Why did that simple statement hint of a double meaning?

Maybe it was because a minister said it. Regrouping, Landon got back into his comfort zone. Schmoozing was second nature to him.

"Erica Monroe, it's good to see you again," Rossi said to a middle-aged white woman whose eyes sparkled. "I would like you to meet Landon Thomas. He has relocated to St. Louis. He worked at Foster & Wake ad agency in Boston."

The woman lifted a brow. "Is that so? I would love to see your portfolio. I've seen their work on national accounts—ingenious concepts. I have some small projects coming up, and I would love to chat with you about ideas." She pulled a business card from her purse and handed it to him. "How can I reach you?"

Landon swallowed. He didn't have business cards or a cell phone. "I—"

Rossi stepped in. "He doesn't have all his contact information situated yet, but give him until the end of the week—until then, call my office." He winked and the woman blushed.

"Stop flirting with me," she fussed. "I'm old enough to be your mother."

"I love my mother," Rossi teased as Erica was called away.

"Thanks for the rescue." Landon slipped his hands in his pocket. "That was smooth."

"Brothers have to stick together." They bumped fists. "I'll have my secretary order you some business cards."

When Landon convinced Rossi he could take it from there, they split up. Casually, Landon snacked on the hors d'oeuvres and used Rossi's spiel about his business cards as he introduced himself. A few minutes later, he spied Octavia looking his way. Instead of acting embarrassed that she had been caught, she smiled and gave him a thumb up.

He winked. Yes, it was a flirt, but it came as second nature. In spite of Rossi singing her praises and Landon thinking such, he wondered about Octavia as he worked the room. Was she the real deal with the Lord or playing church and playing hard to get? Despite his own antics feigning a Christian, Landon would be crushed to find out that was the case with Octavia. There were die-hard saints of God, but he couldn't bring himself to be one of them.

Yet, Octavia had sparked something within him. For once in his life, he was conflicted whether to act on his attraction—and there definitely was one—or to ignore whatever she stirred in him (and it wasn't all raw desire) and keep moving as far as possible from the East Coast and with his history with women, including one in the church.

"God is not mocked. Whatever a man sows, he'll reap," his mother fussed after the ultimate scandal divided the family. "People aren't play toys, especially God's chosen. Mark my words, one day you're going to want something so bad from God and it's going to cost you. I'm praying God spares your life." Lydia Miller Thomas threw up her arms and walked away. Judging from the scowl on her face, she had cut the umbilical cord of mercy on him, and Landon had felt the incision.

The flashback had come so swiftly that he had forgotten he was in the midst of people. He had played church so long with a recurring star role that he didn't know how to be the real deal. His heart had become stone.

Repent, God whispered.

Landon shook himself. This definitely wasn't the place for a come-to-Jesus moment. This time when the server strolled by with champagne, he lifted one off the platter. His hand shook as he tried to take a sip. "Forget it." He stopped after a couple of attempts.

Rossi reappeared as the crowd thinned. "Ready to head out?" Landon could only nod. "Let's say goodbye to Octavia."

Still discombobulated, Landon held back as Octavia smiled at them.

"How'd you do, sis?" Rossi smiled back.

"I'm glad I came. I handed out all my business cards and received some in return. Hopefully, the Lord will give me favor."

"Do you want to join Landon and me for dinner?"

She pouted. "Sorry. I already told Terri I'd be the third wheel with her and Andre." She rolled her eyes. "But I'll see you Saturday at the tent revival."

"Unless the rapture comes," Rossi replied.

This time, Landon was glad they hadn't pulled him into their conversation. Although Rossi hadn't technically invited him to dinner, Landon wasn't going to turn it down. Mac's Place was one of the nicest shelters he had stayed, and meals had been tasty, but he wasn't ready to go back and be reminded that he no longer had the privacy his condo once offered.

"Landon," Octavia said in a tone that seemed to drip with honey. "Please think about coming."

"I'll be there," he said without thinking. When Rossi gave him an odd expression, Landon knew he had just eaten his words. Right now, his fight with God was gone. He was too exhausted. When Octavia was out of ear shot, Rossi smirked and nudged him.

"You're so going down."

"Yep," Landon bobbed his head. "I'm thinking the same thing." As they walked out together, Landon wondered what he was getting himself into.

Octavia beamed then turned around when a woman called her name.

10

Octavia wasn't the third wheel at dinner after all. When she walked into Joe Buck's restaurant with Terri and Andre, a tall gentleman stood and waved them over to the table.

"That's James. Isn't he cute?" Terri whispered into Octavia ear.

"Yes, very," she mumbled. As a matter of fact, he became better looking with every step she took.

He shook hands with Andre and kissed Terri on the cheek while never taking his eyes off her. "I'm James." He had a nice smile. "Terri, you told me your friend was pretty, but that was an understatement." He took a deep breath and exhaled, then patted his heart. "She's breathtaking."

Octavia thanked him as he pulled out her chair.

Moments later, the hostess appeared and asked for drink selections. "Sprite for me," Octavia said as the others requested something stronger.

As she hid behind the menu, she could feel James's eyes on her. She was at somewhat of a disadvantage. He knew more about her than she did about him and he definitely had expectations.

When their hostess returned, Octavia ordered a baked chicken pasta dish and a side salad. Handing over the menu, she had no choice but to meet James's waiting gaze.

As long as he didn't peruse her body parts, she would hear him out. However, Terri didn't give him space to say much as she sang James's praises as if the man wasn't sitting there and couldn't speak for himself. He had an impressive résumé.

"Corporate law," Octavia said to be polite when Terri ran out of steam. "That must keep you busy."

"Not too busy for a social life." James's hints weren't subtle. "Terri tells me you stay busy with church." She nodded. "I wouldn't turn down an invitation, if you asked me." His eyes danced with merriment.

Octavia blushed. "Then I guess I'd better ask. The biggest decision is once you're there, will you accept God's invitation to salvation?"

Terri frowned and gave her the evil eye.

"What?" Octavia jutted her chin at her friend. The few men she did give a chance to had come to church only to impress her as their agenda. With no intention of anything more, they lost interest in her and church.

"Maybe." James didn't commit, but he didn't back down either. She liked when a man had confidence...like Landon. Landon hadn't lost his dignity in his cast-down situation.

Terri quickly changed the subject and kept changing it until their food arrived. James seemed content watching Octavia's every move.

After eating half of her cheesecake, Octavia dabbed the corners of her mouth. "Well, I guess I'd better head home. It's been a long day. James, it was nice meeting you. Terri, thanks for dinner."

"James picked up the tab," her friend corrected.

Tilting her head, Octavia thanked him. When she got to her feet, so did he.

"Let me walk you to your car."

Octavia shrugged. "Oh, I'm in the parking lot and it's still light outside. I'll be fine."

"I insist." He waited as she hugged Terri and Andre, then he fell in step with her. "We're downtown and you never know what homeless guy may be hanging around."

Octavia stopped in her tracks. Homeless? Landon was homeless and she enjoyed his company. She held her tongue as she continued walking, then allowed him to continue to put his foot in his mouth. "Maybe you'll consider volunteering at a soup kitchen with me and see that homelessness could be a temporary fate if we all help."

"I'd rather donate," he said, then in the same breath asked for her number as she deactivated her car alarm.

He opened her door, and she faced him. "I'm out of business cards, but I'll take one of yours."

Twisting his lips, James smirked. "I have a better idea. Why don't I program my number in your phone?"

Okay, it was time to stop this surprise speed-dating dinner from going any faster. "James, I feel ambushed here. Give me your card and I'll call you."

He squinted. "I get the feeling you might not ever call."

"Of course I will. I'm inviting you to church, remember? This Sunday…"

James shook his head. "I already have a commitment," he said, then countered with a movie on Saturday.

"I have a street tent meeting." Once she explained what type of church ministry it was, he declined.

"Thursday."

Since when did dating become a negotiation? "I'm conducting a first-time home buyer's seminar. Do you want to tag along?"

"Can't." This time James didn't offer any reasons why, so Octavia accepted his card, got into her car and drove off. "Lord, I'm not saying he's not the one but I'm not impressed." She was looking beyond his good suit. What was in his heart? *Many are called, but few are chosen.* God whispered Matthew 22:14.

How many times had she heard that scripture? "God, please

chose for me a prayer partner for a mate—someone who knows about Your goodness and mercy…Jesus, please open my eyes to see the candidates You've set before me. Amen."

"So what you think?" Terri asked when Octavia arrived at the office for the weekly meeting.

"I think I should be mad at you for setting me up without giving me a heads up," Octavia feigned an attitude before she laughed.

"But you're not because James is handsome, charming, he has a steady income…"

"I need more than that," Octavia said softly. "You know that. I don't want my feelings to be so jumbled up in a relationship that I compromise. Regret is a hard thing to live with."

Their chat was nipped when other agents filed into the conference room for their Monday briefing.

As the broker, Terri kicked off the meeting with praises before she tackled problems. Since her company was the listing agent on the property Landon had gotten into, Terri accepted the blame for not double checking after a contractor said he had secured it. "Okay, here are our current listings. I want to hear why we're not selling them."

Octavia chimed in, "I am going to re-evaluate how I have those two houses in Olivette staged. They're both listed online. I have that seminar on Thursday, so I plan to showcase them."

Terri nodded and faced another agent whose buyer's offer fell through. She brainstormed strategies how to regroup, and before long, the meeting was over and everyone was out the door. Octavia made sure she was the first in order to escape any further discussions about James without knowing where he stood with the Lord.

The next couple of days whizzed by, but when there was a

pocket of free time, her mind detoured to Landon. She bit her lip from smiling.

On Thursday afternoon, Terri was just finishing up a call when Octavia stopped by the office to grab brochures and supplies for the seminar.

"One of my hardest working Realtors. *Tsk, tsk.* Tavie, you could be a broker by now if you'd focus on different clientele."

"I gave up that notion after working here the first year. Besides, the extra fees and license and the liability to be responsible for other agents' mistakes is scary."

"I know your heart is in the right place with these community workshops, but you need to focus on those contacts you made over the weekend and make some real money," Terri said.

Octavia knew Terri was looking out for her well-being and wanted to groom her to be a broker and to open her other agency office one day, but Octavia wasn't driven by money alone. She wanted to show Christ in her life, and helping others was part of it. "I will...I will, but we know first-time home buyers move within five to seven years to bigger homes. The initial step is to be informed."

Having a place to call home was personal for Octavia. She was a product of a loving Christian home in a distressed area in East St. Louis. The home values were low and businesses scarce, but the minute she and Olivia walked through the door from school, she felt loved, protected and happy. Why couldn't everyone experience the same thing whether it was a two bedroom house or a six?

Call her an old soul or a practicing Christian, but it was her responsibility to serve the under-served communities and to help them go from renters to buyers, which was the main reason she joined the National Association of Real Estate Brokers. As long as racism denied a group of people equal opportunities, whether it was in housing, employment or legal representation, there would always be a minority organization that would fight for access. NAREB groomed the underserved on how to qualify for home ownership and stay in possession of their houses.

When she graduated with a BA in business management, she knew she had to encourage and help people climb out of poverty. If that meant a series of seminars on money management in order to qualify for a first home, then she would do it, so Terri's arguments against that fell on deaf ears.

"Well, please be careful going by yourself into the city," Terri warned.

"Always, I'm thinking about asking Landon. Maybe he won't mind tagging along. Who knows? This info may help him get back on his feet."

"You and your charity cases. I don't care if the man is good-looking. Be careful with him, too. He could have been on drugs, dealt drugs, served prison time, run a prostitution ring. He did something wrong for him to fall out of God's graces," she mocked. "The bottom line is he had to make some bad choices along the way."

Octavia waved. "See you later."

"Have you called James yet?" Terri said in a sing-song voice.

"Not yet..." She grinned and hurried to her car. As far as she was concerned, James was an open book; Landon wasn't and that curiosity made Octavia want to get to know him better.

11

Church. Landon huffed. He wasn't looking forward to going, but Octavia was his incentive. Boy, he missed being around her and watching her dance for the Lord. It was as if he had known her for years instead of barely a week and only two days in her presence. How did she get into his head like that?

Rossi had been right. Octavia definitely ruled, because she was taking over his thoughts as he stared out of the empty room at the Tolliver office building. Rossi had a computer setup for Landon to use as his work space for employment searches and to make follow-up calls. Rossi went a step farther and gave Landon tasks: monitor and update Tolliver Design & Construction Company's website. As if that wasn't enough, Rossi's assistant paid him out of the petty cash fund.

Rossi's business partner, Levi Tolliver, had welcomed him with a handshake. "If my cousin says you're a good person, then you're good. We'll have lunch delivered before noon, so don't be shy."

After creating business cards, Landon had busied himself with updating his résumé, using Rossi's office address and an email for contacts.

"Hey, I'm heading out early," Rossi said, sticking his head into the small room. "I'll give you a ride to Mac's."

Standing, Landon stretched. He couldn't believe it was after four. "Thanks."

During the short ride from the Metro East in Illinois across the bridge to downtown St. Louis, Rossi chatted about sports and his family. Landon kept his secrets close. Ten minutes later, he pulled up to Mac's Place and Landon climbed out.

"Call me if you need anything, including a ride to the church street service."

"Keiner Plaza isn't far. I'll walk," Landon said less than enthused. "Thanks."

He strolled inside and scribbled his signature on the sign-in sheet, so the staff knew that he had returned. Landon was relieved to have the room to himself. Grady wasn't there, but his Bible was lying open on his unmade twin bed. He eyed it a couple of times. "Who am I kidding?" He didn't have it in him to repent and mean it. Dropping his head into his hands, Landon sighed. It seemed like his seed of salvation had fell on rocky soil and never took root after all those years of living and breathing in the church.

He shut out the voices in the hall. Things were starting to turn around, right? He was off the street for the next ninety days for sure. He had a place to sleep, hot meals and a friend, so why wasn't he happy with progress?

You knew Me once, Landon, but you didn't glorify Me as God. Neither were you thankful with all I gave you, but you became vain, God whispered Romans 1:21.

It was the same chastisement that had been haunting him since leaving home. Suddenly, he didn't crave the solitude. Leaving his room, the aroma from the kitchen met him halfway in the stairwell.

In the dining room, Landon went through the motions of eating. The meatloaf and mashed potatoes smelled good, but he couldn't taste their flavor as his mind drifted back to Octavia who had endless beauty and a fresh personality, and he had no chance with her. The devil taunted him with flashbacks of the women he had taken chances with, but those outcomes weren't pretty.

Grady appeared with a tray as Landon pushed back from the table. "What's up?" He nodded.

"Nothing new. See you later." Landon disposed of the remains and rinsed his plate, then wandered to the lounge where a couple of men were gathered.

They were enthralled by a tied baseball game that happened to be with rivals Boston Red Sox and New York Yankees. He sighed. That reminded him too much of what he had left behind. Stretching his legs, Landon closed his eyes and immediately Octavia's face and her flirtatious smile greeted him.

The vision seemed to come alive with her dainty voice flittering around him. Opening his eyes, he blinked and looked over his shoulder where he had a bird's-eye view of Octavia in the lobby, chatting with Brother McCoy. This evening, she was dressed in a silk bone two-piece suit and wearing her name badge.

His heart pounded as he cataloged her every movement. *What is she doing here?* he wondered, sitting up straight. Octavia was an animated talker, moving her hands, swaying her body and laughing in intervals. She brought that energy in her praise dance as if she was one with the instruments.

When Brother McCoy pointed in his direction, Octavia twirled around and strutted his way. The killer smile from his memory came alive. "Hi." She sat without giving him a chance to stand. "Busy?"

"As a matter of fact, I am," he answered sarcastically. "No, actually, I'm bored, but seeing you brightened my day"

"I'm glad to see you, too. Want to tag along with me tonight?"

Landon was about to say yes, but then squinted. "I can't do church tonight and again this weekend," he stated. He didn't care if it was going to cost spending time with her.

They stared at each other, a duel, then Octavia spoke first. "It's a first-time home buyer's seminar," she said softly with disappointment in her eyes.

*Great.*_Now he felt bad. He reached for her hand. "Sorry," he apologized, and her smile let him know he was forgiven.

Rubbing his jaw, Landon realized he desperately needed a shave. If he used one of the shelter's disposal razors; he would nick his jaw for sure and was guaranteed to get razor bumps.

Her eyes seemed to follow his hand, then roam over his face. "You looked very nice on Sunday. I meant to tell you."

"Your eyes told me," he lowered his voice as more men came into the community TV room, either to watch whatever was playing on the screen or live before their eyes. Octavia had every man's attention. What about now?" He challenged her for more compliments.

"You look like a man who is coming back to life." She squeezed his hand. "Stop fighting what God has for you."

Landon gave her a pointed look before standing. "You have no idea what I want at this very moment. Give me a sec to freshen up. I'll be right back." He glanced around at the men waiting to pounce on Octavia. "Do you mind waiting in the lobby near Brother McCoy? I don't want to get put out for hurting someone over you."

Her eyes widened in surprise, but she complied. Landon walked to his room with a smirk.

12

"Good. You're alive, so that means you didn't get mugged last night," Terri said, resting a coffee cup on her desk and folding her arms as Octavia strolled through the office the next morning.

"Nope. God protects His own. Plus, Landon provided extra security." She childishly stuck out her tongue.

Shaking her head, Terri *tsk*ed before picking up her cup. "I'm sure that was a sight to see—a homeless man scaring off a mugger."

"Homeless today, CEO tomorrow. With his personality, Landon will rebound. He mingled with the seminar attendees as if he was at another networking event. I believe God will restore whatever Landon lost, and who knows, I might be the agent to sell him a $500,000 home."

Her friend's chuckle turned into an annoying laugh. "I want to see his credit score and be at that closing." She tee-heed some more. "I doubt Kmart would give him a credit card."

"Stop hatin'." Octavia frowned, offended by her friend's remarks. "It's the grace of God that we have a home, job, car and everything else. You don't know Landon's story." She settled at her desk—the small space she rented every month—and pulled out her laptop.

"So what's his story?" Terri lifted an eyebrow.

"Don't know, but I have a good feeling about him. Landon is a fighter, and he'll get back into the ring." Octavia got up and strolled into the small kitchen and placed a sack lunch in the office refrigerator, then scanned the daily message board.

Terri was on her heels. "You have a lot of confidence in a man you know little about. What you see with that man is what you get: nothing. That also goes for James. What you see is what you get."

"Is James paying you a commission to sell him to me or something?" Terri had never been so resolved about any other man she had tried to set her up with.

"Nope. I know a good man when I see one." Terri leaned closer. "If you wanted to, I bet you could have that man eating out of your hands."

A puppy. She smiled. Hadn't she felt as if she was treating Landon like a stray dog the night she left him at Mac's Place? "I'm sure James is everything you say, but Landon is a soul who needs help."

"And I need bridge work, but my dentist isn't volunteering free services. Weeks ago when I teased you about male companionship, I didn't think you would go to the salvage yard and pick one out. I just get a sense he's using you. Didn't you say he doesn't want to go to church? So when are you going to cut him loose? Surely, Mr. McCoy or Rossi could pick up the slack from here."

"Neither does James, but he won't come out and say it. We're done here." Octavia doctored her coffee and returned to her desk. Terri sulked back to hers. If Octavia was a train engine, she would be spewing steam out the stack. She calmed down and said a prayer, then got up and strolled to Terri and waited while another agent asked a question. When they were alone again, Octavia took a seat. "We've been friends for a long time. Let's keep it that way. You've crossed the line with that hurtful statement about another human being. I'll pretend I didn't hear that because no friend of mine would ever say something that demeaning. Now, I'm drawn to Landon for God's purpose, which is unknown to me. I like him as an individual. We may even become friends at some point. As for now, I'm reaching back and praying him forward."

"I just feel you can do better than spending time with him." Terri looked away, contrite. "My apologies." Her eyes teared. "It was a bad choice of words. Sometimes you give so much of yourself away and get nothing in return. I mean, the Bible says the poor will be with us all the time."

"Just so you know, I did invite James, but he had other commitments," she paused. "Don't twist scriptures out of context, T. If you really understood the entire passage, you would know that a poor woman gave Jesus the best she had. Read it for yourself in Matthew 26."

Both of them were saved by the bell when the phone rang and the call was for Terri. Octavia took a deep breath and allowed her emotions to settle. How was Terri to know and even understand that God had a GPS tracker on Landon's soul?

Enough. It was one thing for Landon to occupy her thoughts, but not her day. She had work to do. Back at her desk, Octavia made follow-up calls, including to Frank Lindell from the mixer.

"Octavia, I was hoping you would call sooner than later. I'm meeting some colleagues for lunch, and I would like for you to be my guest," Frank didn't waste time saying.

As long as he didn't try to ogle any of her body parts, which were well covered, despite the heat, they would do fine. "Of course. When?" She pulled out her day planner.

"Now."

"Now?"

"Actually, in about an hour. I'm leaving my office now."

"Okay…" She scribbled the name and address to use the GPS ap on her phone, then ended the call.

As she grabbed her purse and locked her desk, Terri asked, "Where are you going?"

"To lunch."

71

"But you brought yours." Terri frowned.

"True, but I can't turn down a lunch invitation from Frank Lindell at the Algonquin Club Country."

"Ooh." Terri nodded. "No, you can't! That's how you make that Million Dollar Club," she paused. "You know I love you and I'm in your corner?"

"I know," she replied softly, "but every now and then someone needs a friend. Remember that." She waved. "I'm gone for the day. I have two showings later."

As she drove, her mind revisited her argument with Terri. Landon didn't come across as a man who used people. Should she be concerned? A passage from Galatians 6 came swiftly. *Be not weary in well doing: for in due season we shall reap, if you don't faint. The opportunity is there. Do good unto all men, especially unto them who are of the household of faith.*

The GPS guided her onto a two-lane road. A white wooded fence that sectioned off the golf course led her to the entrance of Algonquin Golf Club: private members only. She had heard from other agents that it was considered an elite golf and country club in St. Louis. She saw why and wondered how many African-Americans had been members since it opened more than one hundred years ago.

While checking her makeup, Octavia gave herself a pep talk. She was always on display when she networked, but when it came to judges, CEOs, attorney, and doctors who didn't share her skin hue, she prayed that wouldn't be a barrier, but a blessing. She always prayed Jesus would give her favor with her BA in Business and her MBA.

She stepped out and smoothed any wrinkles on her dress. Her pearl drop earrings and bracelet jazzed up her simple tan dress. She walked with confidence to the entrance and was about to ask for her host when she saw Frank coming to meet her. "Perfect timing. We haven't ordered."

His smile relaxed her nerves as he shook her hand and then led her by the elbow down a short hall to a dining area where the men out-numbered the ladies as guests.

Frank pulled out the chair and took his seat beside her. Once the introductions were made, the server attended to them, serving salads.

"So, dear, when was the last time you attended the National Association of Realtor's conference?" Mrs. Ashen, a retired surgeon Octavia recalled from the introductions, asked.

"Although I'm a member—" She stayed current with its news—"I've never been."

"Oh," another woman at the table said with an expression of disbelief.

"So what's your area of expertise?" Frank asked.

"I'm a realtor, which sums it up," Octavia stated. Not all real estate agents could boast that distinction without being a member of NAR, which was why she paid her dues, but her allegiance was to the National Association of Real Estate Brokers. NAREB was established as the black counterpart when non-whites couldn't join Realtor organizations, which made her proud to be called a Realtist. "I like to build and nurture relationships, so when a friend is in need of my services, I can provide them with the highest level of professionalism."

That seemed to buy her smiles. After a few hours and a couple drinks from her guests, the mood was festive, but Octavia had to go back into the city to show houses where the sales would barely pay her booth rental at the office.

"I'm having an afternoon tea tomorrow. I would love for you to come," Mrs. Ashen said.

Octavia tried to tame her excitement, so she wouldn't come off as unpolished. This was the open door. Yes! Octavia was about to accept, but she remembered tent revival. Her answer was a no-brainer: being in the hot sun to win souls vs. an air-conditioned party. "I would be honored. However, I have a scheduled engagement tomorrow afternoon that I can't miss." She smiled.

"Another time I hope."

"Let's hope," Mrs. Ashen said in a tone that was hard for Octavia to decipher.

13

On Saturday afternoon, Landon stepped outside and closed the door to Mac's Place. The humidity was waiting for him in the dead heat of the day. "Might as well get this over with," he mumbled as he prepared to walk the mile and a half to Keiner Plaza for the revival under the tent. What had he been thinking not accepting the ride? *Because you thought you might back out,* his mind told him.

His roommate thought it would be cool to go, but in the heat, a tent meeting was anything but cool. "It's my day to spend with my son, and I ain't missing that for nothing. He looks just like me," he said proudly.

Grady's excitement wasn't contagious. Landon tried not to think about being a prodigal father. It was bad enough he was a prodigal son, brother, cousin, grandson, friend...He adjusted the straw fedora he had purchased for two dollars at a secondhand store to keep from suffering a heat stroke.

The hat is not big enough to give you shade. Do you not remember Jonah? God whispered, reminding him of Jonah 4:6. *I give you relief from the sun and shelter from the rain.*

People gathered around the tent came into his view when he

turned on Market Street. It was almost show time as Landon made his way through the crowd; he was surprised to see many of the seats taken. Maybe it was for relief. Suddenly, Landon remembered his hat and removed it. There had to be fifty-plus rows. Landon took the back seat. He would watch Octavia from afar, listen a little to Rossi, then sneak out unnoticed.

The microphone shrieked as an older woman welcomed the crowd. "Praise the Lord, everybody. Come on in where we have shade and water. Despite the heat, we're going to magnify the Lord." She went through a melody of church songs, slamming on the tambourine to keep rhythm. Where were the musicians? He saw a drum set and a portable keyboard. By the third song, a teenager adjusted the seat behind the drums, twirled his sticks and picked up the beat.

Rossi strolled onto the makeshift stage. There was nothing pompous about his mannerism as he knelt before one of a pair of folding chairs and prayed. Landon sensed Octavia's presence before she captured his attention as she appeared with another one of the other two praise dancers.

When it was their turn to perform, the keyboardist still had not shown up and the drummer did his best with "I Give Myself Away," but it wasn't enough for Octavia to soar. Without thinking, Landon stood and strolled down the side aisle to the front. He situated himself behind the keyboard.

This was for Octavia, he told himself as he nodded to the drummer and they harmonized the song. Octavia's body seemed to come to life. Her dancing was like a drug—he wanted more, but when she and her partner slowed their steps, Landon ended the song.

The crowd roared with applause at their performance as Rossi came to the microphone. Landon was about to tip his way back to his seat, but Rossi held up a hand to stop him. "Thank you, Evangelist Gale, for the songs and Sisters Octavia and Deb for the dance...and our musicians, Brothers Dion and Landon."

Brother? Landon hadn't been anyone's church brother in a long time. As it dawned on him what he'd done, Landon squirmed on the bench, uncomfortable being in a pulpit after all the sins he'd had committed and for which he couldn't repent.

"I'm bringing my text from Luke 15:2–7," Rossi said, forcing him to pay attention. "It's okay, if you don't have your Bible, you can find it using your iPads or iPhones. The passage is a parable about something that was valuable but went astray, got lost, and was rebellious.

"*'And the Pharisees and scribes murmured, saying, This man receives sinners, and eats with them. And he spoke this parable unto them, saying, What man of you, having an hundred sheep, if he loses one of them, doth not leave the ninety and nine in the wilderness, and go after that which is lost, until he find it? And when he hath found it, he lays it on his shoulders, rejoicing.*

And when he cometh home, he calls together his friends and neighbors, saying unto them, Rejoice with me; for I have found my sheep which was lost. I say unto you, that likewise joy shall be in heaven over one sinner that repents, more than over ninety and nine just persons, which need no repentance'."

Rossi closed his Bible and began to pray, "Lord, in the mighty name of Jesus, You are the Great Shepherd and we are Your sheep. Help us to stay with the flock…"

Landon began to perspire, and it had nothing to do with the heat. He was relieved when Rossi said, "Amen."

"I call this a happy text. Sheep aren't the smallest animals, but their instinct tells them there is safety in numbers. That's why they flock. God gives us the same instinct. However, they are easily sidetracked. Over the years, there have been reports of hundreds and thousands of sheep that perish because they're following the leader. Sometimes, sheep do get lost mentally as well as physically. With urgency, the shepherd has to find that sheep before it self-destructs. No matter what trouble the sheep finds himself in, the shepherd—his friend and savior—comes to save him…and Jesus will find you"

Landon swallowed as his heart sank. The Master Shepherd had come for him. He didn't know if that was the message Rossi intended to preach, but God was speaking to him.

"This is your day to be still and let God find you," Rossi said softly, asking everyone to stand. "Landon…"

He jumped, hearing his name.

"Will you play something soft—altar call music?" Rossi gave him a look that conveyed Landon knew what he was talking about, then turned back to the crowd. "All you have to do is repent to God. You can either walk up to the altar or raise your hand, and I'll come to you and pray for you. It's time to let God bring you back to the flock…" Rossi continued to plead. "For those of you who want to be baptized in Jesus' name, we have vans ready to take you to church to the baptismal pools."

The keyboard gave Landon security to keep from raising his hand or walking to Rossi for prayer, but something told him things were about to change. Without knowing it, Octavia had lured him out from hiding.

14

Stunned was the only way to describe Octavia's response to Landon's musical acumen. He had a whole lot more church in him than she had suspected. Returning from seeing off the last baptismal candidates, Octavia walked back into the tent where Rossi remained praying with a young man and Landon was still on the keyboard, playing a soft melody. Wanting answers, she focused on her target and marched Landon's way.

"We need to talk," Rossi said to Landon, intercepting Octavia's path.

Octavia blinked and whipped her head around. Wasn't he just praying for someone moments earlier? And now he had said the very words that were on Octavia's lips, so she could only echo his request. "Yes, we do." She squinted at Landon and placed her fist on her hip.

"I'm first," Rossi countered as Landon watched them.

Octavia folded her arms "Well, I'm after you." Rossi was not only a friend, but a minister of God, so who was she to argue?

Not happy about being dismissed, Octavia marched to a nearby chair, flopped down and waited impatiently for her turn. As she gnawed on her lips, she watched Landon's body language as he and Rossi where huddled together near the keyboard.

Who was Landon really? He played the selections as if he were the choir director. God had told her Landon needed rescuing, but judging from what she saw tonight, Landon wasn't a random soul Jesus was calling to salvation. He was a lost sheep that the Shepherd was recovering as in Rossi's sermon.

Octavia waited and waited until only a few people stirred inside the tent, picking up litter or stacking folding chairs. Rossi stood and walked over to her and took a seat. "Sister, this may take a while. Why don't you go on home? Brother Sam can escort you to your car."

"Minister Rossi, I'd rather stay. I want to know what's going on with him."

"You won't tonight. Whatever is on your heart, I'm sure it will be there tomorrow." He stood and returned to Landon who hadn't looked her way.

As if he had been summoned, Brother Sam came to her side and offered to walk her to her car. Reluctantly, Octavia gathered her things. Before stepping out from under the tent, she took one final look at the two men who were in deep discussion.

The drive home did nothing to calm Octavia's heart. She was flustered, confused and angry. The angry part came from feeling "used" like Terri had said, which was ridiculous. Besides treating him to a meal and taking him to Mac's, she had done very little for him.

She arrived home on autopilot. Parking in her garage, she got out and walked through the door. Octavia disarmed her alarm and dropped to her chair at the table. She sat there motionless. Her house was quiet, but the chaos going on in her head seemed loud enough for her neighbors to hear.

Finally, she stood and grabbed her purse. That's when she noticed she had two missed calls from Olivia. Octavia sighed. It was about time her sister called her back, but at the moment the only person she wanted to talk to was Landon. She would play phone tag with Olivia later.

She showered, hoping to wash away the confusion along with the perspiration from the heat. Afterward, she moved through her home with no destination in mind. She was restless—a snack, movie or book couldn't pacify her. She backtracked to her bedroom and knelt by her bed. Octavia had a lengthy petition before God to understand why she felt like an injured party in a relationship that didn't exist. She hadn't realized that she had dozed until her back stiffened from the awkward position. "Amen," she whispered then crawled into bed and turned off the light.

The next morning, Octavia woke early after having a fitful night. She reasoned if she hurried, maybe she would have time to drop by Mac's Place before church and get an abbreviated version of Landon's stunt the previous night. Putting her plan into action, Octavia showered and ate a simple breakfast of oatmeal. Although she wasn't feeling the whole makeup regimen, she applied blush and lip gloss since she did have a showing after church. Her attire was a colorful flowing print skirt and peach sweater.

Octavia itched to call Rossi, who was probably either at his own church or on the way, for any tidbits about Landon's past. It was a silly notion, because as a minister, Rossi took confidentiality seriously. She got behind the wheel of her own car and seemed to make it to Mac's Place in record time. Octavia put on a smile and walked into the lobby. Brother McCoy stopped what he was doing and greeted her.

"I'm hoping to speak with Landon," she said calmly.

"Oh, you missed him. He left about an hour ago."

Frowning, Octavia felt her heart sink. "Did he say where he was going?" She tried to pump him for information without coming across as desperate to find him.

"Nope." Brother McCoy shrugged. "I would guess maybe to church, judging by the tie he was wearing, but he avoids worship service here, so I doubt that." He paused, looking perplexed.

"He might surprise you. Thanks." She walked out the door thinking Landon was becoming more mysterious by the moment.

15

Landon sat in the pew at the church Rossi attended, thinking about Octavia. She had been on his mind since the night before. His heart ached, knowing once he told her everything, he would lose her, not that he had her. Landon wished he could change his past.

A middle-aged, dark-skinned short man with a booming voice got his attention from the pulpit. He identified himself as Pastor Yancey before he welcomed guests. "Before I read my text this morning, I want you to consider this: Have you ever wondered how David, with his sinful, lustful and out-of-control self, could be a person after God's own heart? It just doesn't make sense to us," he said, patting his chest. "God saw something in David hidden from our view—his heart." He paused and flipped through the pages of the Bible. "So my sermon today is 'It's Time for Soul Searching.' Jesus doesn't have to put up with our foolishness. It's His grace that we're not consumed.

"Mark 8:36–38 says, '*For what does it profit a man to gain the whole world, and forfeit his soul? For what shall a man give in exchange for his soul? For whoever is ashamed of Me and My words in this adulterous and sinful generation, the Son of Man will also be ashamed of him when He comes in the glory of His Father with the holy angels."*

Landon bowed his head. He needed that same mercy God had given David

The previous night, Rossi had forced him to do some soul searching of his own. Landon rewound the scene in his mind. He didn't have to stay after Rossi finished preaching, but he couldn't move. As the line grew longer for prayer, Landon kept playing and thinking and eventually praying. By the time Rossi made his way to him, Landon was ready to unload his burdens.

"What's your story, bro?" Rossi said it in a low-key manner as a friend and not in an intimidating voice of a minister who had just preached. "Those church songs were engraved in your heart. I'd venture to say that you're a prodigal son."

"Try a prodigal son, cousin, grandson and father." Landon held his breath as Rossi eyed him.

"I wasn't expecting the last part." Rossi frowned. "Your secrets are safe with me. How many children? Talk to me," he pressed.

Landon looked away. He couldn't face the man of God. No matter how Landon phrased it, he would not come off as endearing. "Four. I slept with women, including one in my home church, knowing that I didn't love them. They knew it too. If they got pregnant, perhaps on purpose, once the DNA testing verified it, I paid child support rather than play their when-to-visit-or-not games."

"The blame doesn't all fall on your shoulders. The devil seems to plant one or two Jezebels in the church," Rossi said as if he was trying to downplay what he had done, but Landon knew himself. He was fully to blame.

Landon had to confess this, even if Rossi wasn't operating in his minister capacity. "There's more…God has whispered James 1:15 to me more times than I can count with a tag line for me to repent." He exhaled. "I was on a path of spiritual destruction that I couldn't get off; it seems like since I was a kid. My cousin,

Garrett, was also causality. Although out grandfather loved us both, I was always the one being reprimanded. I competed with Garrett for the sport, whether he participated or not. When he got engaged...I'm ashamed to say I flirted with his fiancée until she slept with me."

He glanced at Rossi for a reaction, but his face was unreadable, so he continued. "When Brittani became pregnant, she had to come clean about our affair. Garrett hadn't violated her like I did, but she wasn't a virgin either. To save face, she pleaded with Garrett to spare her the double humiliation. He refused...and I didn't love her, so of course marriage wasn't an option for me either. Brittani's recourse after delivering twin boys was to threaten to keep them away from the family. That was a major blow to the Miller clan where the girls outnumber the boys nine to one. The stress had been too much that Grandpa Moses suffered a heart attack." Landon choked. He had been a horrible person and the more he talked about his deeds, the more he hated himself.

Rossi gently slapped him on the back, then rubbed his neck. "It's all right, man. Who am I to judge God's servant? We were all born in sin. That's why we have to repent and be baptized in water and God's spirit. That is the only way."

"I know." Landon nodded. "There's more," he said as Rossi removed his hand. "I was so forgone that I didn't realize I had picked up demons along the way. Garrett's new girlfriend discerned them when I recklessly brought a false prophet to the hospital to pray for my critically ill grandfather." Landon sat there, listening to the rhythmic sound of crickets. With the crowd dispersed, everything seemed surreal.

"Anything else?" Rossi asked.

Landon grunted. "Haven't I done enough damage?"

"The cross is stained with our dirty deeds. God has nothing but compassion—" He held up his finger—"unless you try and play Him. That's what repentance is for, so I'm going to pray for you, because your actions caused a crack in your spiritual armor. The devil widened the gap and invited a slew of demons with a mission to destroy you."

"Yep." Landon looked down at his linked hands. "I thought about ending it all when I lost my job, condo and car..."

"That was the angel fighting for your soul. It's time to turn your life around. Repent—"

"I feel like I'm too far gone. I wonder if my sorry is genuine enough. I've been compared to Esau and maybe I'm more like him than I realize. He couldn't repent either."

They both paused and watched as a couple of men transported the remaining stacks of chairs to the vans, then Rossi turned back to him. "Hebrews 12:17 said 'Esau found no place for repentance, though he sought for it with tears.' Boo-hooing doesn't impress God if a person isn't sincere. Jesus can restore you, if you want to be restored, but in order for that to happen, you need to give your life back to Christ—not only read, but meditate on the Word, come to church and listen to God."

"Oh, trust me, God hasn't stopped talking to me, although I've tried my best not to listen. I guess I'd better start."

"Good." Rossi stood. "Let's get out of here."

"I appreciate you listening and not judging me. The Bible says to 'judge yourself,' and I've done that. I don't like what I see."

"You have a free ride to church, if you're committed," Rossi offered.

"I've got to. God has my attention." As they walked to his car, Landon stopped in his tracks, and Rossi gave him an odd look.

"What?"

"Octavia..." Landon rubbed his jaw. "I have the nerve to be attracted to a godly woman and I don't know what to do about it."

"There are Jezebels in the church, and there are Octavias who really love God. She may seem naive, but she has the favor of God on her life and wisdom." Rossi paused to thank the workers along the way, then turned back to Landon. "If you're the one who God has for her, then I pity you more than her. Remember a rose is delicate, but it still has thorns. Octavia won't allow you to hurt her. And to be honest, neither will I."

Landon respected Rossi for saying that. "Besides not having anything to offer her, once I tell her, she'll hate me."

"Nah." Rossi reached in his pocket for his car keys. "Octavia's going to kill you."

"Run for your life because the devil is on your heels!" Pastor Washington's shrieking jolted Landon back to the present and sent shivers down his body. "This is your altar call. Don't look behind you because it will only slow you down. Look ahead to Jesus who has His arms stretched out. As a matter of fact, it's been that way for a long time. Get up from your seats. Make that change today."

It was time. Landon eradicated whatever amount of pride he had left in his heart to stand. With no turning back, he marched to the front of the church and confessed he wanted to rededicate his life to Christ. Two ministers laid hands on his head and shoulders and prayed. Closing his eyes, Landon saw a vision of Christ nailed to a wooden cross. Rebellious tears sprung from nowhere and flowed down Landon's face.

In spite of the activity going on around him, Landon felt alone and stripped naked before God. Then voices seemed to surround him. Landon realized the entire congregation was rallying behind him. Shouts of "Deliver him from the devil's bondage," "Make his way straight, Jesus," "Give him a clean heart..." The cries of help on his behalf became deafening.

Finally, the Lord's voice pierced through. *Your slate is clean. Now serve Me.*

Everything was a blur after God spoke. The hugs, handshakes and words of encouragement were overwhelming as Landon tried to compose himself. The burdens of his deeds were gone. He felt spiritually cleansed.

"To celebrate new beginnings, let's eat," Rossi offered and treated him to dinner.

Hours later back at Mac's Place, Landon was relieved that he had the bedroom to himself. He even welcomed the sight of Grady's open Bible. Landon stood over his roommate's bed and peeked at the scripture Grady had underlined: Jeremiah 31:3: *The Lord hath appeared of old unto me, saying, Yea, I have loved thee with an everlasting love: therefore with loving kindness have I drawn thee.*

Landon nodded with a smile. "Yes, You have, Lord."

Stretching out on his own bed, Landon fingered his new prepaid cell phone, pondering his next move. Rossi had made sure he had it to make and receive business-related calls. Slipping it out his pants pocket, he stared at the device. After a sigh, he punched in one number he couldn't forget. With every ring, he choked. Finally, before the third one was complete, the familiar voice answered.

"Hi, Grandpa." Tears returned and flooded Landon's face as if he was a lost child instead of a thirty-three-year-old man. He never recalled crying this much as a toddler. He was a man, yet surrendering to God had sucked the life out of him.

Your old life, God whispered. *I'm giving you new life.*

"Landon?" Moses Miller asked for confirmation.

"Yes, sir. It's me."

Silence, so Landon waited to see if he would receive or reject him. There were very few people in his family he hadn't crossed, but his maternal grandfather had been long suffering with his antics. When he issued the ultimatum, Landon realized he had lost his last ally.

"I've repented." It was a prodigal-son moment that his entire family had been waiting for. They had warned him continuously that he needed to repent, but he mocked them, preferring his lifestyle of destruction and self-gratification. He bowed his head. His elbows were anchored on his knees.

"Landon, Landon, Landon," his grandfather said in a cautious tone. "God knows I want to believe you, but your mockery of seven times seventy leaves me suspect. Why don't you tell me what's going on with you?"

"I deserve that," Landon admitted, then began to chronicle his life since being forced out of the condo his family knew nothing about to roaming city to city: New York, Chicago and now St. Louis as he was making his way to Texas.

"Are you ready to come home?"

The cliché "home is where the heart is" was true, but he had to find his heart before he could be at home. "Nah, Grandpa. I'm at a place in my life where I'm starting over. I can't live in Boston anymore."

Moses was silent, which made Landon wonder what he was thinking. "That's your decision alone to make, but you can't make a new frontier every place you go. Women desire love and respect. Haven't I proved that with your grandmother—fifty plus years of marriage—then your parents? You'll never be able to love a woman until you love God first and then your own soul."

This time, Landon let his grandfather's wise counsel sink in—something he had never done before.

"I know that now. I met someone, and God knows I don't want to mess it up."

"Does this young lady know about your past?"

"Not yet—"

"Let's pray," his grandfather cut him off, and without any preliminaries began to call on Jesus until Landon ran out of minutes.

16

Octavia would never grow tired of seeing souls repent. It was the highlight of any church service.

As she watched in awe, souls flocked to the altar for prayer or baptism. Landon's shaved face flashed in Octavia's mind. What was his story? *If he was here, would he be in that line?* she wondered. Once she was finished with her house showing that afternoon, Octavia would pay Landon another visit.

After the benediction, Octavia had only enough time for a sandwich from a drive-thru restaurant. With her immediate hunger quenched, she directed her attention on the Colemans. They were first-time home buyers with demands that were unrealistic.

She and her colleagues preferred listing a property. Other agents besides her would show the home, which would increase the chances of it being sold faster and with less work on the listing agent's part. As a buyer's agent, Octavia was solo. There would be a lot of legwork to get the Colemans into a house they would call home.

The couple didn't have a lot of money to spend; the commission would be lower and after the agent's rental fee to the broker for office space, training and materials, the agent was lucky to have lunch money, which was the reason Terri was always hounding her about changing "the company she kept" to upper-end clients.

The Colemans' loan had been approved for a ninety-thousand-dollar home and not a cent more. Unfortunately, they were adamant about seeing a house with a listed price of $102,000. They didn't want to live in the city, but could barely afford residence outside the city limits.

Octavia believed in options, which was why she dropped by the office the day before to print three additional listings. She had been surprised to see James's Benz parked outside the agency the day before and even more surprised at the conversation she overheard as she neared the entrance.

"James, be patient," Terri stated.

"I have been, but she hasn't called." James's deep voice was a tie between disappointed and annoyed.

"Tavie fills up her social calendar with church activities," had been Terri's defense. "We can double date again."

"No. She was like a mouse caught with cheese last time. She has to want to get to know me. She's sexy, beautiful and the type of woman with just enough church in her to take home to meet my mother…"

Octavia frowned and mouthed *just enough church*. Was that a compliment? That was akin to someone wanting just enough of Jesus to get into heaven. She shook her head. People who didn't go to church and folks who did never would understand the others' reasoning. The bigger question was how much of Jesus did James have. She didn't have time to find out as she fumbled with the knob to alert them that someone was coming in.

Their heads whipped around. Despite their smiles, guilt was written on their faces.

James stood. "Octavia, hi. Terri said you were stopping by. I hope you'll let me treat you to lunch."

"I'm sorry. I'm in a hurry." She eyed Terri then proceeded to her corner desk to print out the alternative listings.

James followed, grabbed a chair and pulled it to her desk. "Why won't you give me a chance to get to know you?"

If Octavia told him that for some unexplainable, foolish reason, Landon had gotten her attention first, he would have laughed.

"What is there about me that you don't like?" He toyed with her as Terri pretended to be busy. To any woman, he was the complete package with his looks, suave personality and other possessions. Plus, he smelled good, but she wanted a man to share her passion about Jesus.

And Landon would? A voice came from nowhere.

"I don't know you," she said, then decided to print out one more listing she hoped she wouldn't have to show.

James had handed her another one of his cards and leaned closer. "Call me any time and I'll answer." Standing, he smiled at her, and his eyes sparkled. He turned and saluted Terri then strolled out the door.

"Girl…" Terri fanned herself. "If you don't go out with him, I may have to leave Andre."

Octavia laughed. "Your husband's not going to let you go anywhere."

A day later, Octavia still didn't know how she felt about James's description of her. *Humph.* He wasn't her problem. She turned down the street where the house was listed and parked. Although she was prepared to hold the Coleman's hands throughout the process, Octavia prayed she wouldn't have to show them ten homes before finding them their affordable dream home.

Her clients honked when they saw her drive up. Octavia unstrapped her seatbelt and got out.

"Excited?" She greeted them and grinned.

Before going inside, the trio inspected the curb appeal, which made a big difference in the asking price. There wasn't much to the flower bed, but the shrubbery was expertly trimmed and positioned for shade.

At the front door, she punched in the combination code on the lock box, which dislodged the key. She opened the door and allowed the Colemans to step inside first, then together they explored the three-bedroom home, which had been fully renovated. It would make a great home for someone with the right income.

Octavia read their body language. Mrs. Coleman beamed. "We want it. Can we make them a lower offer?" Her husband wrapped his arm around her waist. They were a united front, staring at her.

"We can try, but if someone comes with a high offer—"

"With God, all things are possible," Mr. Coleman said.

"Amen." She couldn't argue against that. She knew firsthand about faith, miracles and God's rich blessings. Still, there was a difference between "I want" and God saying, "You'll get." After Octavia slipped a contract out of her case, she suggested they pray.

"Lord, in the name of Jesus," Mr. Coleman began, "You said if we acknowledge You in all things, You will direct our path."

"Jesus, You also said that if we come to You believing... We have been good stewards with the money You've given us..." his wife added.

Octavia was touched by their faith in God. She also knew by helping them to get blessed, she would be too, and she wasn't talking about the commission. Octavia ended the prayer with Ephesians 3:20, *"Now to Him who is able to do far more abundantly beyond all that we ask or think, according to the power that works within us. In Jesus' name. Amen."*

"By faith," they said in unison as if they were the Three Musketeers.

They sat at a table with four chairs that had been part of the few furnishings staged to give the appearance of a home, then Octavia began to write their offer. "The property is paid for and the owner is in a senior citizens' home. Let's see what her relatives have to say." They nodded, stood and shook hands. As Octavia locked up, she knew the hard work was about to begin, negotiating with the seller for a much lower price.

First, she had other business on her mind as she got in her car and drove to Mac's Place.

Half an hour later, she parked in front of the building. She only had one question for Landon. Clearly, he was reared in the church to play those melodies, so what happened between him and the Lord? Getting out her car, Octavia's heart pounded with each step. It was her second visit to Mac's Place in one day.

Another staffer at the front desk instructed her to sign in before pointing to Landon in the common area, tucked away in a corner and reading a Bible. As she crossed the back of the room, Octavia felt the other men's eyes on her. Creepy. She shivered, not wanting to imagine their thoughts.

Landon looked so intense that she felt conflicted about disturbing him, but she needed answers. "Hey," she said softly.

When he glanced over his shoulder, his face glowed. Something had changed within him that was seeping out. He appeared relaxed.

"Is now a good time to talk?"

Landon stood and pulled out a chair. "It will never be a good time to talk about my past, especially with you."

She didn't sit. "Are you hungry? I'm starved. How about grabbing a bite to eat with me?" she rambled on.

"I'm not hungry, but we do need to talk." His expression gave her no clues what details he would share. "Let me put this Bible in my room first."

She was relieved when he escorted her back to the lobby to wait, away from the prying eyes.

He returned in no time. As they walked to her car, she said, "I'm glad you're reading your Bible."

"Me too." He opened her car door.

"I came by this morning, but you were gone," she said, fishing for information as he got in and clicked his seatbelt.

"I attended church with Rossi," he said, reaching for her hand. "I repented and God reclaimed me."

Relief draped her as she chanced a looked at him. "Welcome home. I'm sure the angels in heaven were rejoicing over your soul."

"Amen." Landon choked and shook his head.

She could only imagine the jubilation of being reclaimed. Octavia hoped she never experienced it. She had been in seventh grade when the Lord called out to her. Her classmates were testing the waters in all kinds of things and encouraged her to do the same. God had spared her from life-altering mistakes. She couldn't repent fast enough, get baptized in Jesus' name soon enough and receive the Holy Ghost quickly enough—it was her Nicodemus born-again experience.

Octavia and Landon were lost in their own thoughts until she drove into Chili's restaurant's lot.

"I'll get your door." Landon got out and assisted her.

The host greeted them and showed them to their table without a moment's wait. Octavia declined a menu and ordered her salad and water. Landon asked for a soda.

Once they were alone again, Octavia sighed and folded her hands. "Start from the beginning and tell me about the Landon Thomas I don't know," she coaxed.

Landon looked away, then stared into her eyes. "I come from a large family of Christians who follow the Apostles' doctrine that Jesus taught them. The Millers—my mother's side—has preachers, musicians, Sunday school teachers and anything else in service for God. If I didn't hear the Word at church, I heard it at home or at my grandparents' house. I fought against it."

"That explains your command of the keyboards," she grinned.

"It's your fault," he argued. "I had to see you dance, but I don't want to get sidetracked. Rossi said his sermon on the lost sheep was already planned. I had read that passage and heard that sermon preached over the years, but when Rossi brought it, it stung because I knew I was reaping what I sowed." He inched his hand across the table and chanced pulling one of her hands toward him. "May I?"

When she nodded her consent, he squeezed her hand and Octavia's skin tingled. "Before I tell you what I sowed, Octavia, you have to believe me that I am no longer that practicing sinner, but a redeemed saint."

"Okay." She nodded, but her mind was creating all kinds of scenarios: drug dealer like Terri had implied, embezzlement, outlaw...

Landon's shoulders slumped and he rushed, "I have children..."

Blinking, Octavia sat up straight. She sucked in her breath and slowly exhaled. "Child-ren?" He nodded. "Are you married?" she stuttered.

"No."

Was that the right answer or the wrong one? Her heart and head couldn't agree. He watched her intensely. She opened her mouth and had to force out the next question. "Are you going to marry her?" Why did that question make her heart ache?

He gritted his teeth and glanced around the restaurant. "Three women have my babies." *What?* Octavia felt like someone had slapped her or maybe she was going to faint. Her head began to spin as his voice seemed to echo. Maybe she was dying. She closed her eyes, so it would be quick.

"Hey," Landon said softly, coaxing her to open her eyes. "I'm ashamed, because I knew God's way and ignored it." Before bowing his head, the shame was visible on his face.

Somehow Octavia had a hard time believing Landon could be so callous—her Landon. Her hands shook as she began to wipe at the tears she couldn't control. "Am I your next target? If you have truly repented, then I expect your honesty."

"You never were." It was the first time he smiled and gave her a tender look. "I knew you were hands off when I saw you. It was as if you were under God's protection. I saw purity in your spirit and knew you were the real deal, and that attracted me to you."

Landon reached over and wiped at her tears. "I'm so sorry. I never wanted to see you cry. If you don't hate me now..." He paused as their server placed their drinks before them, then her salad.

"Enjoy," the woman said with a tentative smile, giving them a strange expression.

Octavia doubted that now. Her stomach was warning her not to feed it. If Octavia had to force feed two bites, she had to put something inside her before she did pass out. She closed her eyes to bless her food, but found herself praying for Landon and the women he'd victimized. When she heard him say, "Amen," she opened her eyes. "I wasn't finished."

"I'm sorry."

Staring at her Caribbean salad, Octavia picked up her fork and toyed with the bits of pineapple. "That was deep. I can't phantom how a person—how you—could be that cruel."

He that has no sin, let him cast the first stone, God whispered as in a dare.

She took a deep breath. "Okay, okay," Octavia spoke to the Lord aloud. "I guess you'll be returning to Boston soon."

Octavia watched Landon stalling as he stirred his straw in his glass of Sprite, but he never took a sip. "I was a fornicator, liar, deceiver, and any other name you could conjure up that described me."

Why isn't he answering my question?

He patted his chest. "But this one thing I know for sure, *I would have fainted, unless I had believed to see the goodness of the Lord in the land of the living.*"

Octavia recognized that as a verse from Psalm 27.

"Some things I can't make right. One of those ladies who bore my children—twin boys—was engaged to my cousin."

"You mean she was once engaged to your cousin?" she asked.

"No. They were engaged at the time."

She was done. Her fork missed her mouth. If Octavia was a violent woman, she would have fork-whipped him in lieu of pistol-whipping him for everything. His whorish ways in God's house, his innocent babies, and his family betrayal seemed to put him at the top of Satan's list.

"Is everything okay?" Their server re-appeared.

"Can I have a to-go box, please?" Octavia reached into her purse for her wallet. Not only couldn't she digest her food, but her soul couldn't digest what Landon was telling her.

"No, I've got this," Landon said. The woman looked between her and Landon, then hurried away to do her bidding.

They stared at each other. *Judge not, lest ye be judged.* The scripture revolved in Octavia's head, but how could she not? When God saved her, Octavia was determined to be saved for life. When others around her were dabbling in sin, she and her sister were too scared to explore.

She knew some Christians struggled with issues, but Landon's past actions could only be described as horrific. How could another human being be so cruel knowing Jesus could return at any time and they could be lost forever? Her brain was hurting as she stood. "Let's go."

Landon never cared what others thought about him—until that moment. Never before had disappointment in a woman's eyes cut him to the core, rendering him defeated. If he needed anyone to believe in him…*God, please let it be Octavia.*

"There's no excuse for what I've done. My conscience had been seared, but the Blood of Jesus is my defense, and my redemption has been restored. If I could take back every deed I did, I would," he said softly. He never knew condemnation could be this painful.

Ministers, including Rossi, had anointed his head with oil and prayed mightily. However, the release from his bondage didn't seem to come until God released His Word through a heavenly langue in other tongues that flowed from Landon's mouth. The experience had left him spiritually exhausted and conscience free, until now—again.

When their server returned with the bill, Landon swiped it. "I got this," he said again, referring to the tab, but wishing it also applied to his life.

He trailed Octavia outside and watched as she got into her car, shooting him daggers that didn't need his assistance. Briefly, Landon wondered if she was going to give him a ride back. He jumped in before she gave it much thought.

The ride was surreal until Octavia pulled to the curb in front of Mac's Place. She didn't even look at him when she said goodbye with finality in her voice.

Landon chanced another look at her, but she refused to meet his eyes. He unstrapped his belt and stepped out. His heart twisted at the thought that he might never see her again. "Goodbye, Octavia. Thank you for leading me back to Christ."

17

Octavia had barely closed her front door when the gush of tears started covering her face. Placing her keys and the food container on the counter, she dragged her body into her living room and flopped in a chair. So many emotions flooded her mind. Little by little, she had begun to like Landon, not as a charity case, but as a man she admired, rising above his circumstances. She barked, "What a joke." His confidence had been nothing more than pride. And to think she preferred his company over James. That was another joke on her.

She shivered as the thought of becoming one of Landon's victims, despite his denial, made her cover her face and sob in earnest. Was she playing into his hands without knowing it? Her cell vibrated in her purse, but she ignored it. There was no way she could hold an intelligent conversation the way her head was pounding.

Octavia exhaled when it transferred to voice mail, but it rang again. Getting up, she rifled through her purse and eyed the ID— Rossi.

Yes, she needed his prayers. Taking a deep breath, she sucked in her tears and answered as her voice cracked.

"Sis, are you all right?" Rossi paused, as if giving her time to respond, but Octavia was numb. She tried to nod yes, but her head shook no. No words were forthcoming, so Rossi continued. "Landon called me," he said tenderly. "After I prayed for him, he thought you might need prayer as well."

"Did he tell you…" she hiccupped.

"Yes, everything." Rossi's voice was soothing.

"I was beginning to really connect with him. What am I supposed to do with that information?"

"What do you want to do?"

She said the first thing that came to her mind. "Kill him. Seriously."

"I thought you would, but think this through, Sister Octavia. Landon repented, and God forgave him. Now he needs to forgive himself and resume his rightful place in God's kingdom."

Octavia heard Rossi, knew of Landon's salvation report, but it still didn't mend the ache in her heart. "I was foolish to be attracted to him," she said, making the moment about her. She couldn't help herself from acting this way.

"God has redeemed him," Rossi repeated.

"I wish I didn't know what God had redeemed him from." She shook her head in disgust. "A womanizer. I'm trying to wrap my head around that person. I can't understand people that intentionally abuse others, whether physically or emotionally."

"Yes, the sins Landon committed were horrific from our viewpoint, but the Lord loves him, and Landon knows he has to make restitution and I'm not talking about monetary to his victims. He has to rebuild trust. I plan to be there for him. He's going to need a friend."

Yeah, that's easy for you. You're not a woman. Rossi must have been privy to her thoughts, because he pressed on.

"I'm sure as a woman, it's heart-wrenching, but unless Landon has made any offending remarks or gestures toward you, consider the wounded soldier who has been abused by our common enemy—Satan—on the battlefield and left for dead..."

Only after Rossi began to pray, did the chaos in Octavia's heart begin to settle. "Amen," she whispered softly. "Thank you." Feeling better, her appetite returned. Getting up, Octavia walked back into the kitchen and uncovered her salad.

"You're welcome, *friend.* Remember, this is just as much of our trial as his. He needs us to pray him through this. I believe God has withdrawn his hand of affliction upon Landon's life in spite of the terrible things he did as He had Cain, putting a mark on the first murderer's forehead that served as a warning sign not to harm him."

Octavia remembered reading that passage in Genesis 4 and she marveled at God's mercy in verse 15.

"So now it is on us to do our part as required in Second Corinthians two, verses six and seven. Landon's punishment is sufficient. So now, whether he offended us or not, we must forgive him and comfort him unless he becomes overcome with so much sorrow that he'll never truly believe he is redeemed."

Guilt was beginning to prick at her heart. "When I dropped him off, he thanked me for bringing him back to Christ."

"Believe his intention," Rossi advised, and moments later, he ended the call.

As she rested her elbow on her counter, she picked at the remains of her salad, considering everything Rossi had said. Basically, as a practicing Christian, the ball was in her court. Groaning, Octavia got to her feet and tossed what was left of her meal into the trash bin. She was drained. Yes, she could forgive Landon of his past because he didn't hurt her directly, but what about the mother of his children, his cousin and God knows who else who was in the path of his destructive nature?

"Enough." Octavia rubbed her temples. She had to regroup so she could email the Colemans' offer to the listing agent. Once that task was done, she took a long shower, then prepared for bed with a heavy heart. On her knees, Octavia prayed God would allow the

Colemans' offer to be accepted by the sellers, then she prayed for Landon's restoration and her heart. Once she began to call out the different crises in the world, her issues seemed frivolous. She whispered, "Amen," and climbed under the covers.

Although Octavia willed her body to sleep, her mind wandered. She had made it no secret to God and others that she wanted a Christian man for a mate. She had waited patiently, believing and trusting God that the perfect man for her would walk into her life.

Maybe, she should have been more proactive and put the "church sister formula" into action: sisters would bring their dates to church, willing beaus would repent, be baptized and God would fill them with the Holy Ghost. Soon after that, wedding vows would be exchanged. While many had a happily ever after, some split as if they were recovering from a morning-after hangover. "Nope," she dismissed that formula. That was too much work. She rolled over and shut down her mind.

Unfortunately, the next morning, Octavia woke with an active mind with visions of Landon in the jungle hunting for female prey. She hadn't realized she had cried in her sleep until she glanced in the mirror and puffy eyes peered back at her.

It took some time, a lot of determination, makeup and prayer for Octavia to get dressed for work. The weather was sunny and mild—perfect, except it did nothing for her mood as she was the last person to arrive at the office for their Monday meeting. If her makeup didn't hide her heartache, then she probably resembled a crack addict searching for more drugs.

"Whoa." Terri's eyes bucked as she jumped from her chair. "What happened to you?" Not waiting for an answer, she shoved Octavia out the small conference room before other agents could catch a glimpse of her.

Terri squinted, then twisted her lips. "I've never seen you this disheveled, even lounging at home." She folded. "Give me the Cliffs Notes of what happened after I saw you on Saturday."

Octavia shrugged. She loved mother-hen Terri, but she

couldn't share this, not when it was about Christians misbehaving. "I'll figure it out," she paused. "I signed a contract yesterday." She displayed a winning smile and hoped it reached her eyes.

"That's not going to work with me. Once this meeting is over, we're going out for an early lunch and talk."

In the conference room, Octavia garnered stares. The bright spot in the meeting was she was the only one with a signed contract. Once the briefing was over, Terri made good on her threat and steered Octavia out the office toward the car. Terri drove the short distance to Einstein Bros. Bagels. Terri ordered for them, then claimed a spot.

Leaning on the table, Terri folded her arms. "Okay, spill it. What are you trying to figure out?"

Octavia picked at her napkin. She should have called her younger sister for advice. At least Olivia had good experiences with dating.

"Tavie, you're scaring me." She reached and rested her hand on Octavia's arm. "You don't have to go into details, but tell me something, and I'll pray for you."

Octavia blinked. Her friend didn't say that often, so Terri must be really concerned. Suddenly, she wanted to cry again. "Landon recommitted his life to Christ this weekend."

Terri gave her a strange look. "Ah. Isn't that a good thing?" She tilted her head; confusion was stamped on her face. "What does that have to do with you?"

"I learned something about his past that I'm trying to come to grips with."

"Honestly," Terri threw her hands up in the air as a server placed their orders in front of them. "I don't understand your fascination with the guy. Granted, he's hot, but he has nothing to offer you...unlike Jam—"

"Don't go there," Octavia stopped her. "Let's bless our food." She said grace for both of them, then picked up her ham-and-cheese bagel. The appetite she didn't have earlier was now waiting to be fed. "I'm done with Landon Thomas."

Terri's eyes widened with excitement. "Does that mean you're going to let James step up to the plate?"

Octavia couldn't believe she was about to cave in, but at the moment, she felt defeated. "Maybe."

"Hallelujah," Terri teased until Octavia scowled.

They ate in silence until Octavia took the last sip of her grape juice. Her cell phone buzzed, alerting her to a new email. She scanned the subject line: *Coleman offer rejected.*

"What is it?" Terri frowned.

"The Coleman offer was rejected. I'm not surprised, but I was hoping God would intercede on their behalf." She dropped her phone back into her purse.

"I'm surprised you gave them false hope. It was against all odds in the first place." Terri cleared her throat. "I'd better get back to the office." She stood and gathered her trash. "Clear your head, then give James a call."

It wouldn't be today. Octavia was still going through Landon withdrawals.

18

"Are you going to be all right?" Rossi asked Landon as he peeped his head into the makeshift office.

"Yeah," he said it, but he wasn't so sure. The bus had dropped Landon off at the office a few hours ago, yet he had accomplished very little on the Visitors Bureau project that Rossi had been able to secure for him. He rubbed his hair. After work, he would take a trip to Crowning Glory in Tolliver Town for another shave and haircut at a minimum fee and tip.

"My life is so messed up." Landon shook his head in disgust. "I'm starting to see the magnitude of my mistakes."

Stepping farther into the room, Rossi patted him on the shoulder. "Let's take one day at a time. Despite everything in your past, God has your back; I have your back…"

There was one more name he craved. "Octavia?"

Rossi stuffed his hands in his pants pockets. "Women take mistreatment of any woman personal, so it was a hard pill for her to swallow."

"I know." The thought of not having Octavia as his cheerleader was more devastating than losing anything else in his life. Landon felt an unexplainable spiritual connection with her that he had never felt with any woman. The intensity frightened and soothed him at the same time. His whole emotional entanglement with Octavia started day one as if God had injected him with an Octavia IV drug when Landon hadn't been aware.

He shifted in his chair. Now Landon understood reaping what he sowed. "Well, I guess I'd better tweak this campaign, so I can send it to the client."

"Yep. Remember, this is about *you*. God tracked you down for a purpose. Everything will work out. It may not be overnight, but it will in the end." Rossi backed out, closing the door.

Landon hoped so. "Get yourself together, man," he chided himself. Chasing women got him into trouble. He didn't see how chasing another one would get him out of it. He returned his attention to the graphics for the city's winter promotion. If the Visitor's Bureau liked his ideas on this small project, they could open the door for steady employment in the coming months, which in turn would mean him settling in St. Louis, or should he still proceed with plans to move to Texas?

Later that evening back at Mac's Place, Landon opted for the tranquility of the patio after dinner rather than in the community TV room. It was still hot, but with September on stand-by, it was enjoyable with low humidity. He finished reading some scriptures, but instead of comforting him, Landon had never felt so alone, more than when he was living in the streets.

Generations of his family had served God, and church was weaved into their lives. Yet, there was no gospel music playing in the background, or his mother's humming in the kitchen or his younger cousins reciting Bible verses. There was nothing around to remind him of his rich spiritual inheritance, which he had tossed away.

Landon slipped the pre-paid phone out his pocket. His hand itched to use it, but with fifty minutes remaining, Landon had to ration each call until payday on Friday. He would actually get a check at the end of the week for three hundred dollars—a far cry from his two-thousand-dollar weekly income, but it was money in his pocket and he would pay tithes on it—the first time in a long time. Staring at the card, Landon craved to hear a familiar voice. He reasoned he could spare ten minutes, punching in his grandfather's number

Moses Miller's booming cheerful voice greeted him after the first ring. "It's good to hear from you. How's everything?"

Not as I would like it. "I'm reading my Bible and taking one day at a time. I'm still living in the shelter. I'm doing a little contract work while job searching." He rambled on to get the most out of his call.

"Why don't you come home? Your grandmother and I will pay for your plane ticket," he offered.

Landon smiled. His grandfather was always generous. "No, grandpa. I can pay my own way, but it may be months down the road. Plus, I'm sure nobody is forming a welcome party to see me." At the moment, Landon was sinking into a pity party, which was so unlike him. He glanced at the time. He had already used five minutes and had barely said anything.

"Well, try to make it sooner or later. Brittani made a surprise appearance at church to show that she was engaged and made a special effort to introduce us to her fiancé. The Lord knows I'm praying for her, but the young man appears to be decent. I'm not sure if he's a practicing Christian, but I hope he loves her and will *take care* of the boys."

Right. Landon grimaced. The twins were his responsibility. Until he lost his job, he paid child support, even if he didn't try to establish a father-son relationship with them. Landon rubbed his head in shame. For the sake of his children, maybe he should have played the games the mothers wanted to play about when he could visit, how long and where he could take them, but his tame couldn't be tamed, not even by the mouths he fed.

"When I pulled her aside after church and shared that you had turned your life around, she sneered and refused to believe any words coming out of your mouth," his grandfather paused. "Forgiveness comes easy with the Lord, but expect it to be a struggle with man. But the blame isn't all on you. She was just as much a part of the act while engaged to your cousin.

"Since Garrett's wife is an attorney, she advised we sue for grandparent visitation rights. You know, I don't believe in taking saints to court to settle matters, but I don't believe Brittani has fully repented. Rejection causes bitterness, and I don't want to lose contact with my great-grandsons or the others. After your other children surfaced, we tried to reach out. The only mother who is receptive is Reba, Alyssa's mother. But this is only when we reach out to her. Now, Cherie's mother is a piece of work. I can't get past her profanity to reason with her, especially after you went missing."

With Kim, Cherie's mother, it was more about the missed hefty child support payments he could no longer afford. When he lost his job, he cut back on that until eventually there was nothing. "What a lowlife." He didn't realize he had mumbled aloud.

"Yes, we are without Christ in our lives, but Jesus died for the ungodly, so don't let the devil throw that in your face. Smack him with Romans 5:6. You need to make amends with those mothers first before you attempt to reconcile with the family." He paused. "Your parents and I reared you to be a man, so take care of those responsibilities. If you need anything, you call me, understand?"

"Yes, sir." Lance checked the time. He was already two minutes over. "Thanks for forgiving me."

"Always, grandson. You're my blood and offspring. The promise of the Holy Ghost was made to me, my children and as many generations as the Lord has called, and God has called you as in Acts 2:39. Your mission should be to strive to be a man after God's own heart. It takes faith."

Yeah. His measure of faith was so minuscule that nobody, including Landon, could see it. They said their goodbyes after his grandfather said a short, but heartfelt prayer, then his lifeline was gone.

More now than ever, Landon appreciated his grandfather being his one-person pep squad. No doubt, other family members had a wait-and-see attitude about his sincerity. Landon couldn't blame them. But the one person who Landon wanted to believe his change was genuine was Octavia.

Slipping his phone back into his pocket, he gripped his Bible again. Before he flipped through it, Landon stared out into the yard. Trees shaded one side of the fenced-in property. Some men had planted a vegetable garden in the corner.

His grandfather had told him not to beat himself up. That was easier said than done. Landon had no felt shame in messing around with his cousin's fiancée at the time. He and Brittani had gambled and lost—Garrett wouldn't forgive her or him. Brittani getting married was for the best if the man would accept another man's children—his boys. Landon frowned. Of all the good male role models in his life, why did he have to be the bad apple in the bunch? He looked up in the sky. "God, was my redemption even worth it?" He sighed.

No soul is wasted, God spoke.

19

How does a woman purge another man from her heart? A few days later, Octavia thought she had the answer. Whether it was a wise choice or not, remained to be seen. After taking a deep, cleansing breath, she made the call. "Were you busy?"

James chuckled. "Octavia," he cooed right away. "I told you that if you called, I would answer. So, does this mean you can pencil me in for dinner, say Friday night?"

At least it sounded like a sultry coo to her. Octavia could use the flattery right now to jumpstart her heart. "I have my praise dance rehearsal from six to eight. You can come..." Octavia paused, thinking about the last man who watched the group's routine, even though she had to drag Landon against his will, but that had been God's will toward his restoration. "We can eat after that."

"Two hours...hmm. How about we also catch a movie or go to the museum on Saturday, then dinner, and maybe a brunch and play on Sunday?"

She was amused he could piece together an agenda like that off the top of his head while dodging her question. "I have a house showing on Saturday afternoon," she countered. Was she negotiating a contract or setting up a date? And with someone whose commitment to Christ was suspect.

"It sounds like you work too hard. I can help ease your burden by introducing you to people with more buying power; that way you and I can have more time."

"That would be nice, but until then, I have commitments to my existing clients." Like the Colemans—they had accepted the disappointing news about the house and agreed to keep searching. Octavia was determined to find them something in their price range. "A movie sounds good." She was also resolved to getting out more in hopes that God had a man with her name stamped on his head like an item marked sold. *Lord, help me to stay in Your will.*

"Good luck." James grunted. "Terri told me most of your clientele are low-wage earners and take up a lot of your time and hand holding, but I would like to have that honor of holding your hand before the weekend is over."

She tried to conjure up the image of strolling through a park, holding hands and exploring a new relationship. When Landon's face materialized, she shut that image down. She cleared her throat. "I'm open for anything after church on Sunday. You're welcome to attend. My group will be the praise dancers during morning worship. Will you come?"

"Sure." He didn't sound upbeat. As a matter of fact, she heard an underlining tinge of annoyance.

"James, this is my personal invitation to Jesus the Great Shepherd Church for you to accept or decline. Be upfront with me."

"I am. Shall I pick you up?" Instead of giving him her home address, she gave him the church's. "Octavia, this can work between us, but it's going to take some compromising on both our parts to get to know each other. Agreed?"

"Yes." When they ended the call, Octavia exhaled. Before the weekend was over, she would find out how much compromising James was talking about. "Okay, I did it," she said as if Terri was in the car with her.

Landon hadn't been too happy about going to church either, but look what God had done, so there was hope for James.

The next morning, Octavia worked from home since she was attending an afternoon fundraiser sponsored by a group of ladies she had met through Frank Lindell. She schmoozed and exchanged business cards with female movers and shakers of Fortune 500 companies, plus doctors and lawyers. After a few hours, Octavia said her goodbyes. Not only was the event a success, but the affair raised tens of thousands of dollars for a village in Central America, and it gave Octavia ideas about spearheading a fundraiser for homeless families in America.

On her way home, a man whose side profile resembled Landon caught Octavia's attention, but he was thicker and not as good-looking. That sighting sparked musings of what might have developed between them. She realized her physical attraction to Landon after she came face-to-face with the cleaned-up version at the mixer with Rossi, and Octavia had taken a second and a third glance.

She compared Landon to James. In the looks department, Landon had the edge. When it came to their wardrobe, James won hands down, because he had the means. Octavia sighed. She had to divert her mind away from Landon, which in turn made her think of the women he'd wronged and the babies he'd deserted. She shivered at his recklessness. Besides, he no longer needed her. He was in good hands with the Lord and with Rossi.

As she drove into her driveway, Octavia waved at her elderly neighbor before her sister's ring tone distracted her. She hurried and parked in the garage, then answered. "Hey, stranger. So you remembered you had a sister?" she joked, getting out and walking through the door to her kitchen. She punched in the code to deactivate her home security alarm and rested her purse and keys on the counter.

"Sorry. The internship got crazy, then I had to scramble to replace a class that was dropped..." Olivia seemed to clock a thousand words per minute without taking a breath. "So what's going on with you?"

"How much time do you have?" Kicking off her shoes, Octavia padded across her hardwood floor to her bedroom. Her pantyhose were the first thing that came off. "Well, I'm going on a date," she said without much fanfare

Olivia screamed. "Yes! Landon...?"

When had her sister become a supporter for Landon? Too bad, because she was about to switch sides. "Ahh, it's with a guy named James Kennedy. He's an attorney, good-looking and..." she scrambled to find another adjective to describe him.

"Oh no. Landon's out of the picture so soon?" She sounded as if she was pouting, then recovered with a huff. "What happened?"

"Well, if you had returned my messages, you would have known what I found out about Mr. Landon Thomas."

"I knew it. He had a *Coming to America* thing going on. What's wrong with him being an heir to royalty?" Olivia shouted as if she was on a game show.

Octavia sighed. "No," she said solemnly as she recounted word for word what Landon had revealed. Reliving the moment had her heart aching, but it was a relief for Octavia to unload the burden that she held bottled. Yet, it was still exhausting. "Terri has been hounding me about going out with James. I'm not a fan of B.Y.O.B., but who knows..." She shrugged.

"Oh, no, don't try that 'bring your own beau' to church stuff," her sister fussed, then she softened her voice. "You cared for Landon. You admired him, looking past his present circumstances— no home, no job, no shower—most women would have dismissed him, but you respected him."

"Do you have to remember everything I say?" Octavia rolled her eyes. "Forget all that. He preys on women, church included! I was probably his next victim!" She wanted to scream at the top of her lungs.

"I heard you say that he preyed—past tense—and repented—

present tense, but for the record, I want to back slap him." She paused. "We've never strayed like that since God saved us, but instead of rejoicing with him, you walked away. Most people have a big dark secret. I hope I never have to share one with you."

When Olivia paused, Octavia jumped in. "Is there a deep dark secret you want to tell me?" she pried. "Besides, you've never met Landon, yet you're on his side."

"I'm on the Lord's side," Olivia corrected. "Landon will have to depend on God to give him grace to reap what he sowed. Now back to Jimmy."

"James," Octavia corrected.

"Unless Jesus says he's the work in progress for you, don't force it. Good-looking men have approached you before and there's a reason they didn't make the cut. Your heart will know if James is the one."

Octavia chuckled. "Listen to my baby sister giving me love advice. Hope I don't have to give it back to you when you're confused about a guy."

"I'll look forward to it." Olivia laughed and so did Octavia.

As if the two were brainstorming a business concept, they went over the pros and cons of going out with James. "I say give Jimmy three dates to determine if he wants you and God as a package deal," Olivia proposed.

Octavia agreed and overlooked her sister giving James a nickname.

Friday afternoon, Octavia hurried home from the office to shower and change into something flirty. She chose a sleeveless flowing mid-calf dress and heeled scandals. Once the rehearsal was over, she and James would enjoy a late dinner.

When she arrived at church, there was no sign of James or an unrecognizable car in the parking lot. She waited in the foyer for a few minutes, peeking out the door. Finally, she headed to the women's lounge where her friends were probably changing.

"'Bout time you got here," Kai said, hugging Octavia.

"Don't mind her," Deb teased. "You know patience isn't Kai's strong point."

"I know." Octavia grinned, then kicked off her shoes and slipped on socks. Once all three were in their practice clothes and prayed that God would be pleased, they headed to the dimmed sanctuary. Someone in the technical booth flashed on the spotlight.

Octavia did a sweep and didn't see anyone sitting in the audience. *Okay, he'll be here,* she coaxed herself, rather than becoming annoyed that James wasn't there. "This is not about him," she mumbled to herself and focused on her task at hand.

After they finished the second routine, she spied a solo occupant in the back row. Relaxed, she waved and he waved back. James was late, but he had come. The only other person who had watched her practice was Landon, and that was by default.

She blinked the memories away to perform the third and final number until Deb stopped mid-step and complained, "We're off. I think we should go through it one more time."

Once they were satisfied that the routine was perfect, Octavia beat them to the dressing room to change. "I have someone I want you to meet." She couldn't wait to introduce James to Deb and Kai and get their take. His appearance had sparked a level of anticipation, and she was excited to be swept off her feet.

"I thought I saw you wave at someone." Deb lifted a brow as Octavia checked her appearance. Unfortunately, when she returned to the auditorium, it was empty. Frowning, she led them to the foyer.

"Maybe he's in the men's room," Deb said as her husband pulled up to the entrance and waved before stepping out the car for his wife. "I'll meet him next time."

"Me too," Kai added. "I've got plans." She grinned and hurried out the door.

Octavia lingered in the hall, waiting. When the men's restroom door opened, Brother Michaels strolled out. "Is anyone else inside?" she asked.

"Nope. Just me."

"Thanks." So where was he? She backtracked to the entrance, wondering if he was waiting in his car, which would not make a good impression on her. When she opened the door, James was walking toward her with a swagger a woman couldn't help but admire. Any attitude she had with his disappearing act vanished as she beheld the fine specimen of God's handiwork. She had been crazy not to call him.

"Hi, beautiful." James smiled. As he stepped closer, his sex appeal was definitely overpowering, but she wouldn't let that distract her. "What are you doing out here? I thought you'd wait for me in the sanctuary."

"I'm just getting here." He handed her a long-stemmed rose.

Her mouth formed an "o" as she accepted his token. Someone had definitely waved at her. It wasn't uncommon for church members who were there for meetings to pop in the sanctuary for a prayer, listen to a choir rehearsal or watch a praise team practice. Octavia was disappointed, knowing that it wasn't James.

"I had hoped you could have watched me rehearse." She wanted to pout, but didn't.

"I'm sorry. I'll make it up to you." He winked then steered her elbow toward a silver Benz.

Octavia gently shook her elbow free. "I'll drive."

"Let me pamper you," he offered, dropping his voice.

Was she being petty to think that he missed that opportunity by being a no-show at her practice? Plus, she took the possibility of date rape seriously. "You can pamper me once we get to our destination." She smiled to ease the blow to his pride when disappointment flashed on his face. "Where are we going?"

"Longhorn Steakhouse?" He waited for her approval.

"Then I guess I'll see you there."

James fell in step with her. "I'll walk you to your car."

Half an hour later, they had arrived and were shown to a booth. James was all smiles and compliments—so many that Octavia blushed more than once.

Their waitress introduced herself and advised them of the special. James ordered white wine with his lamb chops while she chose a crab dish and water.

James frowned. "If you don't want a glass of wine, would you prefer a margarita?"

"Water is fine. If I want anything stronger, I'll order a Sprite."

"Very well." The woman gathered their menus and left.

"You don't drink?" James leaned closer. "Not even a little?" He used his thumb and a finger as a demonstration. "Jesus drank wine."

Octavia refrained from rolling her eyes. She would be a rich woman if she passed the collection plate every time someone said that to her. "I appreciate a man who knows his Bible. I'm sure you know the scriptures that warn against being drunk. Since I don't know my tolerance level, I'm good with following Christ's examples with living holy—"

"Whoa." He held up his hands. "I didn't mean to offend you, and if drinking around you does that, then I'll order water, too."

She smiled. "Thank you, but the only way I will learn the real you is to know about the convictions you live by." She rested an elbow on the table so she could cradle her chin in her hand.

Chuckling, James relaxed in his seat. "My convictions are simple: be positive, treat people fairly and go after what I want." He wiggled his brow, then linked his hands together.

"What about God and church?"

"I believe in God, and I have nothing against church unless the preaching goes over an hour and a half." He paused. "Tell me about Miss Octavia Winston."

"I love God and want Him to lead my thoughts and actions throughout my life."

"But does that mean you can't have a life outside of church?" he asked.

"I'm not married, which means I stay busy with church and work." She shrugged.

He leaned closer and whispered, "I can't believe a man hasn't asked you."

"I didn't say that." Her puppy love in high school didn't count and her first boyfriend in college had retracted the proposal seconds after uttering it, stating he was teasing. "I haven't met the right one to say yes."

James sat straighter. "That's about to change."

Octavia didn't want to encourage James, but her spirit shouted, *Then show me.*

Sunday after church, Landon offered to treat Rossi to a buffet with money in his wallet.

"And I'm man enough to let you," Rossi joked. Once they were in Rossi's SUV, he gave a side glance. "You all right, bro? That was a powerful sermon today."

Landon was taking one day at a time. He had lost so much that he was learning to appreciate what little he had gained. He didn't know if he would ever be on top again. That would be Jesus' call.

"Yeah." Landon nodded. "My soul needed to be reminded to press toward the mark, but sometimes it's hard not to look back, especially when a child's mother is holding my grandparents' visitation rights to my children hostage. I'm going to have to make a trip home."

"When?"

"Soon. Brittani is getting married, and there's rumor that the fiancée will adopt the twins. I need to save a little more money first."

"I can lend you airfare," Rossi stated as if it were nothing.

Smiling, Landon shook his head as he watched the passing scenery. "You've done enough for me, man. My grandfather offered, too, but I can do this."

"Well, whenever you go, I'm going with you."

Landon whipped his head around and stared at Rossi. "You're what? You don't have to do that?"

"That's what friends are for. If you kicked up as much dirt back home as you say, you're going to need a friend. Just let me know when."

"I don't deserve this kind of friendship." Landon choked, then swallowed.

"We have no idea what we deserve, but God gives it to us fairly anyway. He is no respecter of persons. Remember Matthew 5:45. Hey, did you get a chance to see Octavia practice?"

"Yep." His heart pounded. "She has a way of stirring my soul just watching her move to the music that worshiped God. Of course, I sneaked out before she knew it was me. It was perfect timing because the bus was coming as soon as I made it to the corner." He missed her—no, he was falling for her. Could this be love, this soon? Was this the reason why he felt he was dying a slow agonizing death each day that went by with seeing her?

Bowing his head, Landon rubbed his forehead and exhaled.

Rossi frowned. "You all right?"

"Probably not. I think I'm in love with Octavia." He swallowed hard labeling his emotions. "And there's absolutely nothing I can do about it. What kind of man tells a woman he loves her, but has nothing to offer to win her affections?"

"As, a friend," Rossi paused and checked the rearview mirror before making a turn, "man up, bro. Stop your woe is me and go after your woman, but I stand by what I say about hurting her. Don't do it."

Landon nodded. Maybe Rossi was right. It was time to get back in the game. This time he planned to chase the right woman for the right reason—love.

20

James pulled out all the stops: flowers waiting on Octavia's desk Monday morning after a weekend of a movie, museum and church on Sunday.

Now, James was treating her to a mid-week dinner date. "So how was your day?" James asked after Octavia led them in grace over their food. His smile was engaging.

"Actually, I had a great day. God turned a decision around for one of my clients to get the home they wanted. The seller had a change of heart and dropped the price twelve thousand dollars when she learned the couple were first-time buyers."

James chewed, then frowned. "But dropping the sales price will affect your commission, won't it?" When she nodded, he rested his fork beside his plate. "How are you making any money?"

"I have other sources of revenue. Banks request broker price opinions or BPOs, where I do drive-bys and take pictures of the property, determine if the houses look lived in, then give an opinion of the value of the property," Octavia explained as he listened patiently minus a smile. "Plus, organizations pay me to conduct seminars, and I pick up business from those workshops."

Shaking his head, James frowned. "You're piecing together an income."

"James, it's not always about the money."

"It's always about the money. If you were more selective in where you network, you could double or triple your income." He picked up his fork and was about to shove mixed vegetables in his mouth, but paused. "Follow the money. Work smarter, not harder."

There wasn't enough money in the world to buy genuine happiness. She looked him in the eyes. "I'm more than a real estate agent or realtor; I'm a Realtist. Our philosophy is to give back."

He pushed back from the table and held up his hands in surrender. "I don't want to fight. I'm just looking out for you."

"I appreciate that, but I've never missed a house or car payment."

He smiled. "You need a vacation. How about you let me pamper you for a long weekend in Jamaica? You can get away from the stress and just enjoy yourself."

"James, I'm not sleeping with you—"

"I didn't ask you to," he said too smugly. "I can book two rooms, and we can spend time together during the day and sleep in separate rooms."

Did he think she was compromisable? Was that even a word? "Hold it right there." She pushed back her food. "You don't get me, do you? I have a good reputation, and going on a get-away with a man who is not my husband isn't a good reflection of holiness. I'm serious about my salvation." She gathered her purse and admitted defeat. She didn't feel a connection with James and it didn't make sense to force a relationship where there was no chemistry. "Unless you have Jesus, I don't expect you to understand, but I'm not the one for you." She stood despite his protest and walked out of the restaurant to her car.

She went home and cried. Why couldn't a man see her worth? James was looking out for her financial interests, but what about her spiritual interests? Landon flashed in her mind. Had he been just an arrogant, charming man, wining and dining and beguiling silly women as the scripture said? How did she go from James to Landon?

Evidently, James was as stubborn as her, because he didn't try to change her mind. For the next weeks, she stayed focused on selling houses. Terri knew better than to say James's name. Olivia, on the other hand, suddenly found time to hound Octavia about Landon until Octavia called Rossi to check on him.

"Praise the Lord, Minister Rossi," she said when he answered the phone. They exchanged pleasantries before she stated the purpose of her call.

"Landon's coming back to life. He's been an asset to my company the short time he's been here, and he's picked up a few contracts. He's saving up his money to buy a plane ticket back home."

Octavia's heart tumbled as she stuttered, "Home? He's leaving?"

"Only for a few days. He's heading to Boston to right the wrong. It's going to take more than one visit for that, so I'm going with him for moral support."

"I'm going," she spoke, then covered her mouth. "Sorry. I said that without thinking."

"Out of the heart, the mouth speaks. It's all right if you want to come, too. My cousin Levi is tagging along because his wife and little girl want to shop." Rossi chuckled. "But we're going as united prayer warriors on Landon's behalf." He paused. "Why don't you come up to my office in the morning? I know he would love to see you."

"I want to see him, too," she softly admitted.

When she finished the call, Octavia didn't move from her window side chair. What was wrong with her? Didn't she get offended at James's invitation to accompany him on an out-of-town trip? Yet, she invited herself for another man.

She ran her fingers through her curls. "Lord, I'm confused. James is a nice man, but he's not for me. All these years, I've prayed for a man who knows Your goodness and mercy." Landon had abused the Lord's goodness and mercy. "Why do I feel drawn to this man?"

The questions were endless, yet God had not answered. Octavia stood. She had never been in love before or uttered those words to a man, so why did her heart feel as if it was breaking?

As she was about to warm up leftovers for dinner, God's presence seemed to fill the room and Octavia shivered.

Landon is a benefactor of My love and mercy. Consider the Pharisee and tax collector. I look for humility in a person's heart. He was My lost sheep that has been found. The voice of God faded as she digested every word.

She stewed on the revelation as she prepared a salad to go with her leftovers. She and Landon had both started on the same road of salvation, then they took separate paths. Fear and trembling kept Octavia and Olivia within God's boundaries for His protection; they thought that if they did sin, they may not be able to make it back. Landon had been fearless and tested God. "He knows more about His grace and mercy than I do," Octavia concluded. "Yes, Lord, You have redeemed him."

The next morning, Octavia dressed meticulously. It had nothing to do with the seminar she had that night or the afternoon networking event, courtesy of a friend of a friend of James's. She was going to see Landon—something she should have done weeks ago. It took the Lord to give her a better understanding about Landon. Minutes after crossing over the Mississippi River from Missouri to Illinois, she followed the signs to downtown East St. Louis, an eyesore for so long, but the Tolliver cousins were making their mark on the historic city.

She parked in the complex, then gathered her purse and nerves. After taking a deep breath, she got out and walked toward the building, wondering what type of reception she would get from Landon. Would he be surprised after she basically wrote him off the night after he poured out his heart to her?

Octavia greeted Rossi's receptionist before he motioned her into his office. "He's working on a campaign," he said in a hushed tone.

So Rossi hadn't told Landon she was coming. He escorted her down the short hall and pointed to the last door. Before he turned around, he patted Octavia on the shoulder. "Reconciliation takes time, whether it's with God or man. Remember that, sis."

"Right." Octavia measured her steps. Although the door was cracked, she tapped softly before peeping inside. When Landon glanced up, his eyes brightened. The tension she imagined would be between them wasn't there. Landon didn't hide his happiness at seeing her.

"Hi," she said shyly. "Can I come in?"

"Of course." He stood. His work space wasn't big enough for two people. "Octavia—"

"No." She swallowed. "Landon, let me get this out of the way. I'm sorry I judged you. Although I don't like what you did, I'm glad you're trying to fix things."

He smiled and stepped aside so she could have his seat. That's when she noticed the files on his desk.

"You have no reason to apologize. After all the things I've done in my past, I'm surprised anyone wants to have anything to do with me. I took God for granted, yet He still loves me." He shook his head as if he couldn't believe it.

"I can't stay long, and you look busy, but I know you're going home to try and sort things out. I want to go with you—and Minister Rossi and his family. I'm in your corner." She stood and looked into his soulful eyes of disbelief.

He wrapped her in his arms and rested his chin on the top of her head. She melted against his chest. It must have dawned on him what he just did, and he stepped back. "Sorry. I just choked. You don't have to go."

"I know, but I feel my heart should be with you."

Stuffing his hands in his pockets, Landon looked away. His eyes appeared glazed over. He clenched his jaw, then he looked at her again; sadness coated his hazel eyes. "I took a part-time job at Walgreens while I wait on something permanent to catch up on my child support payments. A long way from corporate American, huh? I can barely afford to go, and I can't afford to fly you."

There was no value that could be placed on the contentment she felt at the moment. Octavia reached for his hands. "I know what you have and what you don't. I can pay my own way. There are two sides to Landon Thomas. Your family has seen the ugly side, but I have witnessed the redeemed. I want to be there when you testify. Plus, I'll ask around and see if there are any programs to help fathers with child support."

He swallowed. "I don't deserve...I can't even find words to describe how I feel."

"You will." She glanced at the time. "I'd better go."

He linked his fingers through hers before bringing her hand to his lips where he brushed a soft kiss on it. As in slow motion, a tingle started at her fingers and flowed through her body. She stared into his eyes.

"I'll walk you to the elevator." He broke the spell, but kept their hands connected.

When they opened the door and stepped into the hall, Rossi and his cousin were nearby, acting as if they were preoccupied.

Landon cleared his throat and chuckled. "She forgave me." He grinned as the two gave him a high-five as they passed by.

"But you're not out of the woods, yet," Octavia told him as she pushed the elevator button. "Only time will tell if forgiveness is enough." The doors opened and Octavia stepped in and waved goodbye.

Landon exhaled when the doors closed. Yes, forgiveness takes time, but at least Octavia was speaking to him again. Grinning, Landon twirled around and was met with stare downs from Rossi and his cousin. Neither had moved from their spots. "What?" Landon asked. Where were their smiles and high fives?

"My wife likes Octavia. I wouldn't think about messing her over, if I were you." Levi cracked his knuckles. "She served jail time."

Rossi shoved his cousin. "Would you cut it out?"

Landon would have laughed at the joke, but rethought it as he nodded and returned to his workspace, aka cubby hole, aka storage room. Levi's wife owned Crowning Glory. Karyn was the sweetest little thing with smiles for everyone. He grunted. There's no way she would survive in jail.

The scent of Octavia's perfume lingered in the doorway. "I don't care how long or how hard I have to work, I'll earn her love," he mumbled, thinking about Esau and Jacob once again and Jacob's love for Rachel. Just like Jacob had tricked Esau out of something precious, Jacob had the tables turned on him when he met Rachel, and Jacob was deceived when he married the wrong sister. Yet, Jacob made the best out of a bad deal and so would Landon.

Whatever he had to do, he was ready and willing. The other women in his life had seen dollar signs; he had seen bed partners. At the time, it had been an even exchange. Things were different, though, with Octavia—different from day one. She seemed to see something different in him, and he sure saw something different in her.

He yawned and rubbed his hand over his face. He hadn't worked multiple jobs since he was a junior in high school and was saving money to buy his first car. Funny how the very thing he turned his nose up at was now his saving grace: Walgreens at night and Rossi's company in the mornings.

"God, help me. I just need one good job, even if it's half of what I used to bring home."

My grace is sufficient for you. My strength is made perfect in your weakness, God said, whispering 2 Corinthians 12:9.

"I guess that means no." Landon got back to work

21

One look into Landon's handsome face made Octavia's heart soar. She was still humming and downright giddy by the time she arrived at the office.

Terri squinted as Octavia sat at her desk. "You look happy."

"I am. Everything seems all right in my world." She grinned. "I stopped by Rossi's office and checked on Landon." She rocked back in her chair and waited for her friend's response.

"Not him again." Terri groaned and rolled her eyes. "Please tell me he's not the reason you broke it off with James and turned down a weekend getaway?"

"He's not," she defended. "Actually, there's no comparison. Every man who looks good to you isn't always good for you. James wasn't a good fit for me." She patted her chest.

"I can't see how a homeless man can be your custom fit. He's using you to move in with you. It's part of his charm, and you're gullible enough to let him do it." Terri slapped her hand over her mouth and slowly removed it. She cringed. "Sorry. I didn't like the way that came out."

"Me either." Octavia lifted an eyebrow. "I'm a Christian, rooting for the underdog. Landon is trying to salvage his relationship with his family in Boston. He's flying home next week, and I'm tagging along for support."

Terri's eyes bucked before her mouth dropped open, but the words seemed to be on a five-second delay. "Hold up. You're going out of town with a man who probably doesn't have enough money for a Greyhound ticket, yet you turned down an all-expense paid trip to an island?"

"Terri, if you want us to remain friends, then I suggest you stop acting as if you know what's better for me."

Stepping back, Terri shook her head. Clearly, she was surprised by Octavia's sharp tongue. "I'm not a praying woman, but I'm not about to let a man bring my friend down!" She twirled around and stormed away.

I guess that's one way to get someone on their knees. Taking a deep breath to regroup, Octavia turned on her laptop and logged into Marisnet.com to search for new listings. Despite acting as if it was business as usual, Terri's words stung. Octavia was beginning to make exceptions when it came to men. She dated James, even though he wasn't what she wanted, and now Landon didn't have the kind of stability in his life she needed from a man.

Holding down two jobs, even if they were considered part-time, was taking a toll on Landon. He wasn't a teenager anymore. His body and roommate reminded him of that when he fell into his bed at Mac's Place. However, Octavia knew how to give him a boost in the mornings. He smiled every time he strolled into Rossi's office and there was a card from Octavia waiting for him. It was day four, and she had yet to disappoint him. Thanking Rossi for his mail, he proceeded to his work space to rip it open. *Let the redeemed of the Lord say so. Be encouraged.*

Landon had no right to be in love with her, but he was.

Things were beginning to fall into place when Southwest

Airlines had one of their twenty-four-hour specials a week later on payday. Landon gave Rossi the money to book his flight along with Octavia's. "I can't let her pay for her ticket. I don't care if she's coming of her own volition."

Rossi smirked. "I respect that. I'm glad Karyn is coming, so there will be no evil spoken of against Octavia for traveling out of town with single men. We're there for you, brother," he said, then booked everyone's tickets. "We're all set. There's no turning back now. You ready?"

"I don't think I'll ever be ready to face this army," Landon answered honestly as he walked out the door to catch the bus for his night gig.

22

"I'm nervous," Octavia whispered as she stood next to Landon at Lambert Airport, waiting for security personnel to check their IDs. Landon squeezed her hand, and she responded with a smile. If he stared long enough, Landon was sure he would see a glimpse of her love for him. At the moment, he was searching for it.

Although it was rather early, Octavia was alert. She smelled like peaches, and her attire was casual. Not one curl of her blondish brown hair was out of place until he tugged at a strand. "I know why I'm nervous, but why are you?" He lowered his voice to shut out everyone around them and focus on her.

She jutted her chin and Landon smirked, bracing for a snappy response. "I don't want anybody to mess with you." She lifted a brow in a sign of defiance.

"Thank you." Her honesty humbled him. "Believe me, I can take whatever they dish out. I'm sure they have questioned my DNA to the family, so I have to earn their trust."

"You earned mine." She stepped to the podium and handed the TSA worker her ticket and driver's license.

For a quick minute, Octavia's fearlessness reminded him of Garrett's wife, Shari. Before the woman married his cousin, she wasn't fooled by his church-mimicking antics. Shari had rebuked those devils right out of him for bringing a false prophet to the hospital to minister to his grandfather after a heart attack, which he had indirectly caused.

Looking back, Landon accepted he was on his way to hell with no regrets. Jesus' grace, which persuaded him to repent, was invaluable.

Once his group cleared security and were situated at their gate, Landon observed Octavia as she chatted with Karyn about clothes, hair and other female topics that lost Landon's attention.

Rossi and Levi suggested they take a walk around the terminal to kill time. Dori jumped up. "Can I go with you, daddy?"

Levi smiled and reached for her hand, but Landon hadn't stirred. He was fine right where he was, sitting across from Octavia, but not wanting to come across as a sick puppy, he stood. As he trailed the cousins, Landon overheard Octavia telling Karyn, "Hopefully, I can do some shopping with you, but I plan to stay close to Landon, in case he needs me."

Landon hid his smile. The woman gave him a level of strength that couldn't be measured. It was a spiritual boost that only his heart could feel. Once they boarded their flight, Landon gave Octavia the window seat. As their plane took off, Landon closed his eyes, praying for mercy from those he'd wronged. He had tested the mothers of his children beyond what was humanly possible.

*They will never forgive you...*the devil taunted him.

As Landon rebuked the devil, Octavia squeezed his hand, then she whispered, "It's going to be all right."

Landon's spirit stilled. She was that in tune with him. Opening his eyes, Landon faced her and linked his fingers through hers. "In Jesus' name. I accept that."

That gave him peace to doze until they arrived at Logan Airport. Landon stirred and was surprised to find he had a grip on Octavia's hand. When he met her eyes, she was smiling.

"It's going to be okay."

Landon took a deep breath and looked around as passengers began to gather their belongings. "I have faith in God and hope in God, but that's where it ends." Landon shrugged. "My family may forgive me, but a scorned woman will be out for blood."

"No woman deserves what you did, so I'll be praying that the Lord Jesus gives you a double dose of grace," she didn't try to sugarcoat it.

They got off the plane and made a pit stop to the restrooms. When everyone was ready, Landon led the way to the baggage area. As he exited the terminal, Landon stumbled, but recovered when he caught sight of a small welcoming crew. Some held balloons and signs: *Welcome home.*

Landon had to will his feet to keep moving as his heart pounded. He did a quick head count as his grandfather stretched out his arms. The welcoming gesture was enough to make a grown man cry, but Landon didn't as he loosened his hand from Octavia's and walked into the embrace as if he was a boy again. Once Landon had reached puberty, he insisted on handshakes as the norm, but not today. His pride was gone. "Grandpa."

One by one, his greeters bestowed him with hugs and kisses. Landon was living in the moment until he realized the attention was no longer on him. "Oh, I'm sorry," he said, making introductions.

"Octavia, Rossi, Levi, Karyn and Dori, this is my grandpa Moses, my grandmother Queen, my mother, father and one of my two sisters."

His grandfather stepped up and gave Rossi a hearty pat on the back. "I've heard good things about you. Thanks for being instrumental in my grandson's life."

Rossi squeezed his shoulder. "He's like a brother to me."

Landon had to ask, "Do the others know I'm here?"

His mother didn't make eye contact with him as she answered, "Yes... it's too soon. They want nothing to do with you. Sorry, son."

Nodding, Landon accepted their rejection. He would need a triple dose of God's grace.

Once everyone retrieved their luggage and secured a rental SUV, Landon gave them his parents' address. The plan was for Rossi and the others to check in at the hotel then come to his parents' house for refreshments.

Settling into the backseat of his father's car, Landon thanked his parents for coming. Although they had spoken since he returned to God, they held back, expecting that the old Landon would probably surface. His sister, Zion, was snuggled next to him with her hands linked in his. No one would ever guess by her display of affection that she was five years older than him.

"You're our son," his father stated while his mother nodded. "We still love."

"Your grandfather has called a family meeting in a few hours and advised everyone to be there," his mother told him.

The family meeting, aka Miller tribunal, was usually called when there was bad news to deliver. Landon swallowed. He was it. "I expected as much. Rossi and the others will want to be there."

"Of course." His mother nodded, then angled her body to face him in the back. "Son, I'm glad you're here and you've repented, but this hasn't been easy for any of us. The Miller name is tainted at church, your cousin's ex-fiancée made sure of that before and after she had the twins. Even though she no longer attends our church, the gossip resurfaces every now and then." His mother had aged in the past few years from his ordeal. Although he was fair-skinned like his father, he received his "pretty-boy" features from his mother: long lashes, wavy hair and high cheek bones.

"The devil comes to kill, steal and destroy…" his father mumbled.

"Well, I'm glad Satan didn't destroy you," his mother said. "I'm praying that Brittani will come back to God before the devil causes her to die in her sins."

"I don't need to tell you that being a father is a privilege.

Children have short memories. They take their fathers at face value, willing to remember the good while forgetting the bad. You can still have a place in their life," his father stated as they pulled up in front of their Roxbury home. For once, Landon didn't question his father's counsel, but accepted it.

As they waited for the others to arrive, Landon was the center of attention, but not as the boastful man he once was as he shamefully disclosed all the misfortune that befell him. There were a few sniffs. He decided to wait to tell more once the others arrived. Some would be glad to see him, but probably only because they wanted to hear what lie he would spin this time. He sighed. His reputation truly preceded him.

"Even though I disowned you, I never wanted you to be homeless." His father choked back his emotions.

"Have you reconsidered moving back here? You'll have a place to stay until you get back on your feet," his grandfather said, then offered his home.

He wasn't ready for a big move just yet. "Thanks, but I have a place to stay at the men's transitional shelter. I'm working at Walgreens in the evenings and at Rossi's office during the day to earn enough money for three months' rent. Octavia is going to help me find a one bedroom or a studio. Rossi keeps me busy with real projects for his firm in between assignments while I wait for something full time."

"Do you need help?" his sister asked.

Landon smiled and pulled his sister into a hug. "I got it."

Soon, his grandfather led them in prayer. Landon had always taken moments like this for granted. He was always a spectator when the family prayed. Now his spirit rejoiced as he lifted his voice in praise and petitions. Before long, God filled the room and began to speak to them, filling their mouths with His heavenly tongues.

When the final Amen was whispered, everyone was wiping their eyes, including Landon.

"Well," his mother said, smiling, "I feel better. I'd better warm up the food before more family and your guests arrive."

His grandfather held him back while the others went into the kitchen to help. "I'm not one to mince words. I know Jesus has redeemed you, but the devil doesn't like to let go and give back, so I have to ask about Octavia. She's very pretty. Are you using her, and I'm saying this delicately?"

"No, sir. I'm not." Landon felt so good to confess that. "I love her."

"I see. You're going to have to work extra hard for her." Moses gave him a stern look.

"I know."

"Good. Remember, second chances are never promised or guaranteed."

23

Landon's family was nothing like Octavia had expected. From the moment she and Rossi's family entered the house to a crowded room of at least thirty-plus onlookers, they were received with pleasant greetings and a couple of hugs

She came prepared for chaos, but the atmosphere was jovial. Many seemed genuinely glad to see Landon—or perhaps they wanted to see evidence of his tattered life. Before long, they had an impromptu church service with testimonies of God's goodness and songs of praise.

Octavia said, "I know we've all shared testimonies, but there is one more thing I would like to say." Landon's grandfather consented, so Octavia proceeded while Landon eyed her with a curious expression. Octavia began to perspire as a hush swept through the room. "Thank you everyone for a warm reception." *Deep breath,* she coaxed herself. "I don't know the Landon Thomas that lived here, but I do know the one who lives in St. Louis. He's a good man who has allowed God's Word to take root in his heart. You may not recognize the new man, but I can't see any remnants of what he says he used to be. Please pray for him."

A few mumbled, "Amen."

His grandfather quickly filled the lull. "Minister Tolliver, do you mind sharing a scripture."

"Of course." Rossi cleared his throat and stood. "God has laid it on my heart to remind us of Christ's love for the church in Colossians 1:13–14: *'For He rescued us from the domain of darkness and transferred us to the kingdom of His beloved Son, in whom we have redemption, the forgiveness of sins.'* I can't leave here today without commenting on the reception you all have given Landon who has become like a brother to me." He paused and looked at his cousin. "Sorry, Levi."

"No harm done." Levi smirked as everyone laughed.

"We were all born and shaped in sin, but Jesus rescued us. When we live in darkness, Jesus is the light to rescue us..." Rossi said, summing up his sermon minutes after he began. "Landon's in God's hands in St. Louis. You all have my word that we'll have his back and the assurance that God will supply his every need, according to His riches in glory by Christ Jesus."

"Amen," some mumbled; others shouted and clapped.

As Octavia and the others prepared to leave, Landon grabbed her hand and pulled her to the side.

"Thank you for all the things you said about me, especially the part about me being a good man." He bowed his head, then looked at her again. "I've never been a good man, and to hear someone say I am...you make me want to live up to your and God's expectations."

"Landon, have you forgotten the scripture about being tried by fire?"

"No, I haven't forgotten. It's in 1 Peter 1, and I've been singed."

She couldn't resist reaching up and touching his jaw to see if it was as smooth as it looked. Landon captured her hand with his. "I have no right to say this, but I love you, Octavia Winston."

The soulful gaze in Landon's eyes made Octavia want to cry. His profession tempted her to make a similar declaration, but not yet. She couldn't, and Landon seemed to understand it.

"I guess I'd better let you go. I'm bracing for drama when I meet with the mothers of my children tomorrow. I'm having second thoughts about you coming."

Too bad, she thought as she planted a fist on her hip. "Dear Landon Thomas, this is why Minister Rossi, Levi and Karyn, and I came. Those mothers especially need to see you've changed if you want to have a relationship with your children." She paused. "Do you want a relationship?" She searched his eyes, looking for the truth.

"Yes, I do."

She exhaled. Whether he knew it or not, his answer was the best way to show her his capability to love her. "Good night." When she turned around, Octavia hadn't realized she and Landon had been the center of attention. She blushed.

"We'll be here tomorrow afternoon, bro, to pick you up. Tomorrow is your test," Rossi said as everyone was going out the door.

"Please come early enough for breakfast or brunch," Mrs. Thomas said.

Rossi graciously declined. "Some devils are bound by fasting and praying, so another time?"

"Of course!" Landon's mother said, and his father suggested they all fast and pray the next day.

The family members who were still there nodded. "Consider it done." Their willingness to fast impressed Octavia. When it came to walking as a Christian, her pastor taught her that fasting and prayer worked together for their good.

Back in the rental SUV, Octavia retreated to her own thoughts, which was a rewind of how Landon looked at her when he said he loved her. His words were so heartfelt that they over-powered her senses. In the back of her mind, a tiny voice questioned if he had ever told another woman that.

No, she didn't want doubt to creep in. If he had, then that had been the "old" Landon. Still, her parents didn't rear foolish women. She lived in the Show-Me-State of Missouri, and she was forming a list when they made it back to St. Louis for him to show her.

24

The aroma of bacon, eggs and pancakes was absent in Landon's childhood home on Saturday morning. The only scent Landon sniffed was his shower gel. "Lord, get me through this day—physically and spiritually. In Jesus' name. Amen."

Landon continued to pray after he dressed, and once he was ready, he picked up his Bible to fortify himself with scriptures until his St. Louis cartel arrived, minus Karyn and her daughter who hit the stores in downtown Boston.

His grandparents had arrived at the same time as Rossi and the others. After anointing everyone's forehead with Holy oil, his father led a short prayer before sending them off with the old saying, Godspeed.

"So, which house are we hitting first?" Levi asked in the driver's seat as he slipped on sunglasses.

Octavia gasped from her spot next to Landon in the backseat. "Brother Tolliver, that sounds callous, as if we're going to drug houses or something."

Rossi agreed while Landon kept his thoughts to himself. He had Octavia's hand secured in his. It felt good to have an intimacy with a woman that wasn't physical. Clearing his head, he focused on the task before him. His friends didn't know it, but they were about to cross into dangerous territory. Landon had used these women and tossed them aside. His innocent children suffered.... He wasn't going to rehash that.

I am no longer that man, Satan!

When Octavia covered his fist with her soft hand, he relaxed. "Brittani's." He sighed.

As they drove throughout the city, Landon wasn't inclined to be their tour guide and point out all the historic landmarks of his beloved Beantown. As Levi followed the GPS, Landon's heart pounded when the navigator said, "You have reached your destination."

Landon closed his eyes and took a deep breath before opening his door. He had been missing in action even before he left Boston. When he had contacted the mothers of his four children earlier in the week, he got mixed responses, which was a heads-up to brace for some drama. "Maybe you all should wait in the car—"

"No!" they said in unison.

"Okay," he conceded.

"Although this is a private matter, from what you told me about Brittani, she may be civil in front of guests," Rossi suggested.

Landon didn't argue as they climbed the steps to her home. He felt like he was part of a team of Jehovah's Witnesses about to knock on her door, but they were coming in Jesus' name. When Brittani opened the door wearing a white midriff shirt and tight jeans, he was glad for their presence. Wasn't this woman engaged? He frowned.

She peeped around him. "I thought you were coming alone."

"I never said that."

Twisting her lips, Brittani stepped back and half-heartedly allowed them entrance. Landon watched as Brittani eyed Octavia. "Have a seat in here." She pointed to a room that was tidy, even with toys stacked in the corner. "I was about to change."

Mmm-hmm, Landon thought. He paced the room, nervous to

see his sons for the first time since their first birthday party, which Landon had received an invite to the day before. He took the blame that he hadn't been more involved. Landon should have gone head to head with Brittani, but with everything else going on in the family—that he was to blame—he had picked his battles.

Would Benson and Bryan remember him? Landon stopped in his tracks. Why was the house so quiet? Were the twins even there? His nostrils flared until he caught glimpse of a small photo on an end table. As if he was a military drone locked on its target, Landon walked over to it and picked up the photo: his sons. He strained his mind, wondering if he would be able to tell them apart after all this time.

"They're cute," Octavia said, coming to his side while Rossi and Levi remained seated.

He grinned. "Thanks. Carbon copies of me as a boy." Landon couldn't deny they were his.

Brittani reappeared and indeed, she had changed into something more presentable—clothes that covered her chest and stomach, and pants that allowed her to breathe.

At the same time, keys jingled and the front door opened. A tall man walked into the room and looked at each guest before focusing on Landon. Brittani looped her arm through the man's, identifying him as her fiancé Charles.

"Sorry, I'm late, babe." Charles kissed her on the cheek. "I meant to get here before your guests."

Landon shook Charles's hand, introducing himself and the others. With the pleasantries out of the way, Landon asked, "Where are my sons?"

"The proud papa returns." Brittani snorted, then *humph*ed. "They're taking a nap. Chill. You've waited this long, you can wait a while longer."

"Landon, do you mind if you, Brittani and I speak in private?" Charles waited for Landon to agree before steering them across the hall into the kitchen. Her fiancé seemed like an okay guy. Landon hoped Brittani would appreciate him. "Knowing the boys, they won't stay asleep long." He chuckled.

Landon glanced over his shoulder. Rossi and Levi gave him encouraging nods. Octavia mouthed, "Praying," and capped it with one of her brilliant smiles.

Once they were gathered around a rather large table, Landon silently prayed for guidance.

"I don't think we should relive past regrets," Charles got to the point before Landon could begin his spiel. "So let's start from today. Landon, Brittani says you live in St. Louis now. As a man, I appreciate you stepping up to the plate..."

"Finally," Brittani mumbled as she glanced around the room.

"I paid child support until I lost my job. I explained that to you," Landon argued.

"Don't worry about it, man." Charles waved him off with a shrug. "Babe says you have other children. I imagine that's a heavy burden, but I'm willing to lighten the load."

Why did Landon have a feeling he wasn't going to like it?

"I love Brittani, Benson and Bryan. They need a father in the home, twenty-four-seven. I want to be that man and give them my last name, which means you won't have to pay child support as long as you agree not to interfere with our parenting..."

All of a sudden, Charles didn't seem like such a nice guy as Brittani looked at the man with worshiping eyes.

"Now wait a minute. I don't think you understand," Landon said. "I've lost enough time with my sons. I want in their lives, not out."

Whatever Brittani was about to say, Landon cut her off. "We can go to court to work out the arrangements, but I won't give up my parental rights. I insist on having visitation rights to include a month with me every summer..." Landon really hadn't thought this through, but since this was coming out of his mouth, he had to own up to it. "The judge can determine what I should pay for child support. I'm here to right the wrong in my relationship with my sons. As far as name changing, I will petition the court for my sons to keep my last name."

"It's a little too late for you to make demands..." Brittani smarted off.

Landon hoped Rossi, Levi and Octavia were praying, because he was doing everything in his power to reign in his temper. Brittani had nerve. When Landon informed her that he wasn't marrying her, it was Brittani that had a list of demands that held the boys hostage from his family...and him.

"I think we all agree we want what's best for the boys. I've been here for them; I stepped up to the plate when they needed guidance." Charles patted his chest. We're not ex-ing you out of the picture completely. If they want to seek after their biological father when they reach a certain age..."

"Ah, naw." Landon didn't recall raising his voice, but Rossi, Levi and Octavia appeared in the doorway with concerned looks etched on their faces.

"Perhaps we need a time out," Rossi said, but didn't wait for an answer as he joined them at the table. Charles and Brittani seemed respectful of Rossi's position as they yielded the floor to his guidance.

As everyone calmed down and Levi and Octavia returned to the living room, Landon wondered if Brittani made the boys take a nap at the time she knew he was coming.

"Benson and Bryan are too young to travel to the South since you don't plan to come back to Boston," Brittani stated. "And what about her?" She pointed to Octavia. "I don't want her mistreating my children."

Slapping his palms against the table, Landon gritted his teeth. "The boys are almost three. They are too young to travel alone, so I would accompany them, and I hadn't said I would never come back..." At least he hadn't to her anyway. "Until that time, I'm willing to make trips throughout the year for weekend visits. As far as Octavia, this is not about her—yet."

Octavia reappeared. "Brittani, none of us here are the enemy. Landon has changed, and I believe he'll be a good dad."

Brittani grunted. "I see what's going on between you two. Old Landon's got you believing he's going to marry you, doesn't he?" Brittani said with venom.

"Babe—" Charles gave her a side eye—let it go." He rubbed her hand, which seemed to have a calming effect.

"Marriage?" Octavia blinked. "I believe Jeremiah 3:14 that God is married to the backsliders who return to Him," Octavia said softly, then pointed at Charles as she said to Brittani, "You're getting a second chance at love; give Landon a second chance with his sons, please...please." Octavia disappeared to the living room as the house came alive with bumps, thumps and little feet running down the hall.

Nothing else mattered at the moment his sons appeared in the doorway. Landon's heart soared at the sight. They looked from one adult to the other before going to Brittani and Charles's laps. Landon hid his disappointment. What did he expect?

Landon could feel all eyes were on him as he coaxed his sons to him. Charles said nothing as one of the twin clung to Charles.

Bryan came to Landon out of curiosity and then Benson followed. Before long, the twins led Landon to the living room. When the boys raced to the toy box, Landon got on the floor and played with them. An hour or so later, when Landon announced he had to go, Bryan and Benson begged him to stay. Their pleas were bittersweet. He wanted to stay, but he had two little girls who needed to get to know their father, too.

At the door, Landon shook hands with Charles. "Brittani, you've done a good job with my sons," he complimented and handed her an envelope containing a five-hundred-dollar money order. "This is all I have for them now. I'll send more regularly until the judge decides what I can afford to pay. I'm sorry, again." Next, he squatted so he was eye level with the boys. "Be good and I'll be back as soon as I can."

"Whew," Landon and the others exhaled at the same time once they were back in the rental. "Thanks for being there," he told them.

"Always," Octavia whispered and squeezed his hand.

It seemed as if Landon had just regrouped when the GPS brought them to mother number two: Kim Rayford. Once again, the drama began on the porch at the front door where Kim refused entry to Landon's guests.

"It's okay, man, we'll wait in the rental," Rossi said as the trio walked back to the SUV.

Once inside, behind closed doors and without his friends to act as a buffer, Kim released four years of pent-up frustration as a single mother. "I should call the police and have you thrown in jail..." She started cursing, causing Cherie's tiny voice to call out for her mother.

"Aren't you going to get her?" Landon asked, growing concerned.

"You don't tell me what to do!" She got up and disappeared down the hall. Landon began to pray that God would bring peace into the home. She returned, dragging with her the prettiest little girl. How long had it been since he had seen his second born? Longer than Landon shamefully cared to admit. "Kim, I'm sorry I upset you and hurt you. I'm working to get caught up on my unpaid child support...I would also like visitation rights."

"I'll think about it."

Cherie watched him with curiosity as she clung to her mother's side. Landon concluded that a couple of hours wouldn't be enough time to break the ice to begin the bonding process. They needed more one-on-one time. He thought about the dolls Octavia had purchased for his daughters since he was clueless on what to buy, but he had left Cherie's gift in the car. If he went outside to retrieve it, knowing Kim's mood, she might not let him back in. "Can you show me your favorite toy?"

His daughter nodded, but didn't move. Who said four-year olds were talkative? Cherie was the most reserved child he had met in a long time. With no assistance for any type of transition coming from Kim, Landon wished Octavia was there. She would know how to get his daughter to open up to him. He began to pray for help, but Cherie didn't make a move toward him. Time was up sooner than Landon had wanted, but if he was going to see all of his children in one day, he had to go. Getting to his feet, Landon handed Kim an envelope with a two-hundred-fifty -dollar money order. Cherie stayed close to her side.

Humph. Kim looked inside. "You've got to be kiddin' me. You give my baby crumbles with your fancy job."

"I lost that job. I've been homeless, and now I'm working at Walgreens until I can get back on my feet."

There was no lost love between him and the woman whose relationship was a couple of weeks of hot sex. Kim released a belly laugh that lingered until a tear dropped. "Walgreens?" She laughed until she sneered at him. "Next time, bring me cash!" Kim walked to the door and opened it. Taking the hint, Landon left. His foot had barely cleared the door when she slammed it.

When he climbed back into the SUV, he collapsed against the seat. "What a mess I've made." *Lord, I didn't think it was going to be this hard!* Dropping his head into his hands, Landon slumped over. He had never been so humiliated. Cursing had come easily before, now he had to bite his tongue.

"It's going to be okay," Octavia said softly, rubbing circles on his back. Her touch was soothing.

"We've been out here praying," Rossi said. "Are you up for another visit, or should we wait until tomorrow?"

"Nope. I've waited long enough to see my children, and Alyssa is six, so my visit is long overdue."

Half an hour later, Landon arrived at a small house in Hyde Park. He braced for another mental showdown, but he and his crew received a warm welcome. Although Reba Kee wasn't a practicing Christian, she had no ill feelings. Her husband, Martin, had adopted Alyssa because Landon didn't care enough to protest it, even after the DNA test proved him to be the father. Alyssa was sharp, appeared well cared for and happy. Landon couldn't thank Martin enough for stepping up to the plate and being the man he wasn't.

Reba and Martin had prepared snacks, and Alyssa was eagerly awaiting the arrival of the special guests. The atmosphere was light-hearted.

Landon thanked God for the reprieve. Martin led the men into their entertainment room. Although Landon appreciated the hospitality, he'd rather spend his time getting to know the girl he had rejected from the moment she was conceived.

"No hard feelings," Martin said, opening a can of beer. "I got blessed. Reba and I met when she came to the office and applied for WIC. She was a damsel in distress, and I wanted to be the one to rescue her. I'm a happy man." He grinned and reached out to Reba when she walked into the room with mini sandwiches. Alyssa trailed, assisting her mother as a hostess-in-training. He watched his daughter's every movement.

Looking away, Landon bowed his head in shame. What kind of human being was he to force his firstborn to live on public assistance when he had the means to provide for her comfortably, even if he had no intention of marrying Reba?

Now, he had so little to offer Alyssa and the others, and it went beyond the money. He was thousands of miles away from them. Landon's heart began to ache from cheating his children out of so much—his love and their cousins, uncle and grandparents whom they knew little about. At the moment, he hated himself for his past actions.

I have cast your sins in the depth of the sea, God whispered Micah 7:19.

That reassurance lifted Landon's spirit. He was thankful that Reba and her husband had told Alyssa about him. He would be forever grateful.

He faced Martin and Reba. "As I explained over the phone, I have three other children—a set of twin boys and a younger daughter. I'm not asking for your pity, but your prayers as I try to right my wrongs. I don't have much, but as I continue to bounce back, Alyssa will get more." Landon gave him the envelope with the last three-hundred-dollar money order.

Martin waved him off. "Put it in a college trust fund. Never too soon to save." He reached over Alyssa who had wedged a space between them, and patted Reba's stomach and that's when Landon noticed the bump.

"We're having twins." He beamed.

Landon's mouth dropped, then he blinked. "Wow. What are the odds of Alyssa have twins on both sides? Congrats, man." Landon shook hands with Martin.

"That means I'm going to have two twin brothers." Alyssa beamed.

"Two sets of twins," Martin corrected. "We don't know if they'll be boys or girls, or one of each."

Where Cherie was quiet, Alyssa was a chatterbox as she talked about what she learned in school and about wanting a cat. Landon wanted to stay longer, but it had been a long day. It was time to head back to his parents' house. He, Octavia, Rossi and Levi hadn't broken their fast with a prayer yet before they ate, so they were starved. The snack Reba tempted set before them. Once everyone prayed, then they would celebrate with a feast at his parents' house.

Back in the SUV, Landon was quiet as he processed the magnitude of his responsibility to four children. Should he move back to Boston? Landon had taken family for granted. His cousin Garrett came to mind. He realized he owed Garrett a call and a real apology, but not today.

25

The closeness Octavia had felt with Landon earlier in the day was gone by the time she made it back to their hotel Saturday night. They broke their fast with prayer and thanksgiving at Landon's parents' house, but she could tell by his body language that he was numb as his parents peppered him with questions about their grandchildren.

"I can't..." Landon said, piling his plate with turkey and dressing as if it was Thanksgiving. He was going through the motions, but Octavia doubted he had an appetite after a day charged with emotional baggage. "Sorry, mom and dad, I need to process today before I can even talk about it."

With that statement, he excused himself from all conversation until it was time for Octavia, Rossi and Levi to head to the hotel. "Thanks for being there for me," Landon stated with little emotion in his voice.

Octavia wanted to reach out and hug him and will life back into his body, because the events of the day had literally been sucked out of him.

Days later, Octavia was not the same after returning from Boston, and neither was Landon. The experience left her shaken, witnessing the bitterness, hurt and lingering feelings that Landon had played a hand in. She also saw the hunger in his eyes to reach out and connect with his children. Octavia's heart didn't choose sides. She hurt for all of them.

She was glad she had been proactive in researching agencies to help fathers who were behind on their child support payments, especially after Landon told her about Kim's threat to have him jailed for lack of financial obligations when they were in Boston.

In addition to working like crazy to save up money to send back to his children and pay for another plane fare to visit them, Landon was participating in the St. Louis Chapter of the National Fatherhood Initiative.

The love he professed in Boston seemed to be on hold in St. Louis. Every minute of their time seemed limited. Octavia had begun a routine of sharing lunch with Landon at Rossi's office. Today, they were crowded in his work space, eating Arby's fish sandwiches, which was his treat.

"I can't wait until I finish this two-month Fathers and Families program; then the agency will pick up my back child support payments that totals thousands of dollars. It will give me a second chance to pay from my heart and not because of obligation.

"Not to mention jail. Kim could've made good on her threat to have you arrested."

Landon sighed. "Yes, and then I would have a felony on my record."

He reached for her hand and caressed her fingers. His lips parted, and Octavia waited for something to come out. She didn't notice when he sucked air into his lungs, but his sigh was audible as he shook his head. "Thank you, baby," he said with such tenderness she could see why any woman was drawn to him. "God really blessed me when He sent you into my life."

"And don't you forget it," she teased to mask the fluttering of her heart from hearing the endearment, but Octavia remained cautious. Did they have a future, especially with his recommitted bond with his children?

They hadn't kissed yet, and if and when they did, Octavia didn't want to experience it in the confines of a closet of an office. She busied herself with gathering their discarded trash and stood. "I'd better head out. I have an appointment with a widow I met at a luncheon who wants to sell her home in historic Webster Groves. When we chatted, I had no idea she would be in the market."

Landon got to his feet. "I've been praying for you."

Those words were like saying he loved her. For her, that was the language of love. She stared into his eyes. "Can I ask what you've been praying for me about?"

"For you to reach that Million Dollar Club level; I hope God gives you the desires of your heart, because you're the most giving woman I've ever met outside of my mother and grandmother."

"Now you're going to make me cry," she said, looking away.

"If you cry, I'll wrap you in my arms and kiss you like I love you." Landon didn't blink.

Don't tempt me! Octavia sniffed and backed out of his office. *It won't be here.* "Bye." As she walked away, Landon whistled. She whirled around. He leaned against the door post, folding his arms and grinning like a boy with a new toy. She always thought a man whistling at a woman was insulting. Landon made her feel attractive and...giddy. She playfully stuck out her tongue and hurried to the bank of the elevators.

By late afternoon, Mrs. Kerr signed the contract, making Octavia her listing agent for her historic home. Silently she praised God and thanked Landon for his prayer. The next step was requesting an appraisal on the thirty-five-hundred-plus square foot, renovated two-story, five-bedroom house. Judging from the property value of the neighborhood and what comparable homes sold for, Mrs. Kerr's asking price could be in the upper four-hundred thousand, if not five-hundred thousand.

As soon as Octavia got into her car, she texted Landon the

good news before driving off. *Thank you for the prayers. I got it. I'm heading to the office to do the paperwork!*

Octavia almost floated into the office less than a half hour later. Once her colleagues heard the news, it was pure jubilation in the office. Terri lifted her hand for a high five.

"You've been on fire since you returned from Boston. See, the right connections can make all the difference. Congrats, sis." Terri paused when Octavia's phone rang. "We'll talk later," she mouthed as Octavia answered the call.

She had barely said hello when someone entered the office lobby and slammed the door. Glancing over her shoulder at the offender, Octavia was surprised to see James. Evidently, he had come to visit with Terri, who was across the room, since Octavia had called it quits more than a month ago. She turned her attention back to her caller, but James stopped at her desk. Ignoring his presence, Octavia patiently answered the potential client's inquiry.

"Yes, I do remember you from the seminar a few months ago…Your loan approved for what amount?"

"One hundred and ninety thousand dollars," Mrs. Scales said.

"What area were you thinking about living?"

"My husband and I think Bridgeton and Maryland Heights are centrally located."

"Good choices." Octavia made notes, wanting to engage the buyer in small talk, but Mrs. Scales left her contact number and ended the call. With James's figure looming over her desk, Octavia had no choice but to acknowledge him. "Hello. Can I interest you in some new property listings?"

"I can't believe you," he managed through gritted teeth as he continued to tower over her desk, since she didn't offer him a chair.

She'd had a thing about people talking down to her ever since she was in the first grade. Her teacher, Mrs. Elsberry, stood over her, making sure the entire class knew she had an accident before she could make it to the bathroom. How was she to control a stomach virus? Octavia got to her feet, almost reaching his chin in her stilettos. She tapped her manicured nails on the desk, waiting him out.

Maybe she shouldn't have baited him, but James had made two mistakes, showing up at her workplace with an attitude, then bringing that attitude for a show in front of the other agents.

"Women are always talking about how they can't find a good man, and you had one." He thumped his chest. "But no, instead you go after a bad boy."

She squinted. What is he ranting about? Octavia counted to ten to nick whatever camp fire he was trying to start with two sticks. "Excuse me."

This is a test, God whispered. *Satan wants you to fail and mock Me. I can keep you from falling.*

"I invited you to a weekend getaway to Jamaica with the works." James fanned his arm in the air. "You turned me down like that." He snapped his fingers. "I had time to think about what I could have said wrong. I stopped by the office to apologize that I had been out of line not to respect your choices only to find out you had skipped town with some lowlife—"

"Watch it. Stop right there." She held up her hand as she rolled her neck. "Your tailored suit can't dress up your lowlife mentality. If you're referring to the company I prefer to keep, then it looks like you're going to owe me another apology. Landon has been where you are—past tense. He buried his pride like you should that green suit. His best quality is he has firsthand experience about God's goodness and—"

"And I know how to talk to a lady," Landon's terse voice made heads turned. Where James had made a grand entrance, Landon had quietly walked in. "If you've got a problem with me, step outside. I want to hear it."

Jesus, Jesus, Jesus, Octavia began to silently pray as she walked up to Landon. "Don't do this," she whispered, nudging him toward the door. She turned back and shot James an evil eye, then in one blink, softened her look toward Landon. With little resistance, Landon obliged, but once outside, Landon paced the perimeter around her car and looked at the entrance as if silently daring James to take him up on his offer.

Every stride toward his restoration with God would be tainted if Landon took the first swing. Octavia had let James taunt her, now Landon was falling prey to the enemy. *Lord, help us not to make You ashamed. In Jesus' name, please keep us from falling in the devil's snare,* Octavia prayed, hoping James wouldn't make an appearance until Landon calmed down.

Blocking Landon's path, she reached for his hand to hold him still. "Hey, hey," she said softly. "I like surprises." She smiled.

"I don't." Landon scowled and looked at the door again.

"I'm not talking about James, but you. Please don't let the devil steal your joy. You have nothing to prove. You've done that with God. I made the choice to go with you." James didn't need her, but Landon did.

He grunted and eyed the door again. "The moment I heard a bellowing voice and saw who it was directed at, I made a choice that nobody was going to talk to you like that. Yes, I'm serious about my salvation this time, but that doesn't mean I'm going to sit back and let the devil be the life of the party."

"And what were you going to do, beat James with your fists? He's an attorney—think lawsuit. He could have you charged with assault and battery," she said, trying to reason with him, rubbing his arms. She could feel the tightness in his biceps.

"Would you prefer I use my pocket Bible to beat him down?" Landon didn't flinch.

At that moment, James strolled out of the building. Terri was behind him, and some of her colleagues were gawking out the window. Octavia stood in front of Landon in a weak attempt to hold him back as he and James engaged in a stare-down duel.

"I'm done here," James spat. "I don't have to fight over a woman, especially not one whose standards are lower than mine."

Landon made one step forward, and Octavia dug her nails into his arm to hold him back. "Think of your children. Set an example," she whispered.

He growled before shouting, "Man, you're out of your league. You don't know Octavia's worth. She's one of those women whose standards are so high that any man would fight for her."

James said nothing as he slipped behind the wheel of his Benz and sped off. Octavia put both hands on Landon's face, pulling him away from watching James's tail lights. Once she felt she had his attention, Octavia smiled. "Thank you for saying that."

"I meant that because it seems as if I've been fighting to have you before we even met."

Instead of her heart fluttering, it did somersaults. "You're trying to make me cry again?"

Completely relaxed, Landon smirked. "Go ahead." He taunted her with a nod. "I've got a remedy for that."

Giggling, she glanced over her shoulder as Terri shook her head before stepping back inside. She turned back and softly scolded him. "Humph. I can handle myself. I've got God's protection."

"Hmm." He twisted his mouth and stared at her with so much intensity that she shivered. "He sent me."

She wanted to melt in his arms, but she restrained herself. "Really? God sent you in Minister Rossi's car?" She attempted to joke, but Landon didn't seem to share in her humor.

"When you texted me, I wanted to say congratulations in person, and I was willing to ride on the Metrolink, then transfer on the bus to tell you. Rossi had pity on me and let me use the company car. I have no candy, flowers or—"

"You're the best gift." She stood on her toes and puckered her lips. They weren't in a closet, but she felt he needed to be rewarded for good behavior. He delivered the softest peck that made her want more.

The brief encounter seemed to leave both of them dazed. "I'd better go. I have to work tonight. Congratulations, baby."

Octavia noted his swagger as walked back to Rossi's car. If Landon Thomas had no class, then no class was the new black.

As soon as Landon was out of Octavia's sight, he pounded the steering wheel in frustration. Fighting over a woman was beneath him, but so was begging for spare change when his residence was any available park bench. "Jesus, please forgive me for almost stumbling," he mumbled.

Once his repentance was out of the way, Landon did an instant replay of the scene. His reaction to the other man surprised even him. In his old world, women had fought over him to his amusement, but he had never felt that territorial. He couldn't claim Octavia with nothing to offer—no car, no home, no steady employment to woo her, but she was the exception to the rule. He would beat down man or beast that tried to disrespect her.

But you have her heart, God whispered, reminding him that she chose him over the other dude.

Yes, she made it seem as if it didn't matter and that's what caused him to love her more. That thought kept him grinning until he pulled into the business park where Rossi's company was located. He dropped the keys off at the receptionist's desk and strolled back to his office. With the incident forgotten, it was back to business as usual. He had one remaining project he had to review for a local chain of cafes before sending it to the lead executive on the campaign.

At the end of business day, he and Rossi walked together to the elevator. "So was Octavia surprised by your visit?"

"Yep. Me, too." Landon didn't go into any details. "Thanks for letting me use the car."

Rossi nodded as they stepped inside and pushed the button. When the doors opened, Landon declined Rossi's offer for a ride to

Walgreens for his evening shift. The brother had done so much for him; Landon could never repay him.

In the lobby, they usually parted ways: Rossi veering left to the employee parking lot, Landon going toward the front entrance to the bus stop less than a block away, but this day, Rossi fell in step with him. "Do you have a plan?"

"What do you mean?" Landon kept walking. He had seven minutes until his bus arrived. The trek would take him four, but Landon didn't want to lose track of time if the driver was ahead of schedule. Either they would have to pick up the conversation the next day or Rossi would follow him to the bus stop.

Rossi seemed to do the latter. "I know that trip to Boston was a turning point in your life. Have you decided how Octavia fits into your plans?"

Landon rubbed the back of his neck. "I don't have an easy answer for how to give the children and Octavia equal time. Right now, everything I'm doing is to re-introduce myself to the children as their father. I'm working to pay child support again, to return to Boston to see them…"

"Bro," Rossi looked down the street, "Here comes your bus. Someone has to be a priority. Even in a marriage, the wife has precedence over the children. I'm not saying you want to marry Octavia or she'll marry you, but either way, make a decision and follow your heart." He pivoted on his heel and strolled back in the direction of the building as Landon boarded the bus.

Rossi didn't even have a wife, so what did he know about a woman being a priority? He nodded at an elderly gentleman before snagging the seat next to him. As the bus turned to exit on the Poplar Street Bridge into downtown St. Louis, Landon thought about family again. Landon's reconciliation was in the works in regards to his children, but there still was another wronged party. He had put off contacting Garrett. His cousin called Landon's apologies "disingenuous," and Garrett had been right. Landon had been going through the motions, not taking full responsibility that he had lured Brittani away from her fiancé, preferring to spin the story that Brittani had seduced him.

That night, on his dinner break, Landon would make the call. Garrett no longer lived in Boston, but had relocated to Philly soon after Landon and Brittani's secret was out.

Forty minutes later, Landon stepped off the bus. Walgreen's parking lot was packed, and when he cleared the doors, cashiers manned two registers trying to shorten the long line. He hurried to the back and clocked in. Slipping on his smock, which had his name badge pinned to it, he checked his appearance, then walked out front.

With a new cash drawer in his arms, Landon relieved the weary-looking pregnant woman. "I'm glad to see you," Amanda said and didn't stick around to chitchat.

Customer traffic was non-stop for hours before Landon could take his dinner break. His mother had gotten Garrett's number from his aunt, so it was now or never he decided as he popped in a TV dinner and punched in Garrett's number. His heart pounded, when who he assumed was Garrett's wife, Shari, answered.

"Hello?"

Clearing his throat, he asked to speak to Garrett. Of course, she asked who was calling, and of course, there was a pause when he told her. Although Shari muffled the phone, Landon could hear Garrett in the background refusing his call. Really, what did he expect—open arms as their grandfather had given him? Evidently, Shari won the tug of war and Garrett got on the phone.

"Yes." His cousin made it clear he didn't want to talk to him.

Landon didn't go for the "hey cuz" greeting. He had lost that privilege. "I'm sorry." Garrett was quiet, so he continued, "I was home over the weekend."

"So I heard. I'm glad my family and I don't live there anymore."

"I repented, Garrett—*really* repented. God accepted my forgiveness and chased the devil out of my temple and filled me with His Spirit. I cried and spoke in tongues so long, I was hoarse. As God gives me strength, I'm going to try and be a better son, grandson, brother, father and cousin, if you'll let me."

Unless his family told Garrett about his homelessness, Landon wasn't about to use that as a trump card to garner sympathy. "Anyway, thank you for taking my call—or rather thank Shari. If our paths ever cross in the future, please remember that I've changed."

There was silence, so Landon waited. He had eloquently apologized to the family in the past. This time, he didn't have a prepared speech.

"I'll remember. Take care, cuz." The call was done, but the endearment was remembered.

Landon blinked away moisture from his eyes. Garrett hadn't called him cuz in a long time.

26

"What's the latest?" Olivia asked, waking Octavia from her slumber. Octavia didn't have to ask Olivia what she was referencing. She should have never told her sister about the showdown between James and Landon and the sweet brief—too brief—kiss they shared. Since then, Olivia had been hounding her weekly for an update about Landon as if Octavia's life was a reality TV show. Unfortunately, the lunches they carved out for themselves began to fade with Landon's need to study for his fatherhood class and the increase of luncheons she attended to network with more affluent clientele.

It had been a long day and an even longer evening with the homeowners' seminar. Octavia yawned and eyed the time. Eleven-fifteen. She groaned. She really needed the rest.

"Can you believe Landon completed his father initiative program? That went fast. They had a ceremony for the graduating class last Friday morning and several of us attended. I was so proud of him. It was as if he was receiving a master's degree. Two days ago, a big PR firm downtown offered him a permanent job. We all took him out to celebrate. He's saved up enough money to fly back to Boston next weekend to see his children before he starts." Octavia took a deep breath. She would miss him. "That about wraps it up."

Silence. Silence and more silence. Finally, Olivia mm-hmmmed. "Thanks for updating Landon's bio, but I was hoping for something that included you and Landon." She *tsk*ed her disappointment.

So would she. Octavia stretched and slid deeper under the light covers. She tried not to make any demands on the man who was trying so hard. "Landon knows I'm here for him, but he's putting all of his energy on seeing his sons and daughters. He doesn't have time to invest in 'us'—not now. Maybe never." Why did doing the right thing make her heart ache?

"Can't fault a man for being a man. Are you planning to take the trip again with him?"

"Nah, he's a big boy. I think he's got this." She had to change the subject. "Hey, I do have some exciting news! I'm $210,000 away from making the Million Dollar Club!" That made her giddy. God was giving Landon the desires of his heart and doing the same for her—only she had tweaked her request.

"Go sister, go sis..." They laughed. "So, Landon..." Olivia switched back, and Octavia groaned. "Do you regret loving him?"

Octavia had never told him, but she was sure he knew. She let her heart settle before answering. "No, but Landon Thomas will be a hard act to follow. I can't imagine another man measuring up to him. He knows God in a way I can't begin to comprehend." She sighed. "Maybe one day when I'm telling my nieces and nephews that you're going to give me—"

Her sister shrieked, then laughed.

"Seriously, I'll be able to tell your children about a pure love that came from the heart, no materialistic things to cause a distraction, no lust, no letting others sway you, just putting yourself out there to see if there could be that one fish in the water. No regrets, sis. No regrets."

Olivia said, "I'm glad you're my big sister."

Wiping away a tear, Octavia curved her lips upward. "I'm glad you're my sister, too. Of course, my relationship with Terri has suffered, so I chalk that up as a casualty. There's a line girlfriends should respect."

"That's too bad." Olivia *tsk*ed. "I always thought she had your back."

"Yeah. As long as she thought she knew what was best for me."

"As long as you're all right. If Landon wasn't a father of four, I would hurt him, but those babies need their daddy, so he's safe."

"Bye." Octavia laughed and rolled over. She prayed that someday Landon would be recognized for a father of the year award, because from where she sat in the bleachers, he was sure trying to earn it.

On the day Landon boarded the plane to Boston, Octavia received the congratulations from Terri. "Welcome—you officially have one million and one hundred thousand dollars in home sales!"

Octavia screamed her excitement as tears fell from her eyes. Terri led her into the small conference room where there were balloons, cake, and in her honor, sparkling juice instead of wine. Her colleagues cheered. Rossi was there as well as Deb and Kai, her fellow praise dancers. Octavia shrieked when a surprise guest stepped from behind Rossi.

"Olivia!" She hugged her sister, smothered her with kisses, squealed, then started the ritual over again. They hadn't seen each other since last Christmas. Octavia patted the tears on her cheeks. "When did you get in? How did you know…"

Her sister pointed at Terri. "Your friend redeemed herself." Terri joined them in a group hug. Octavia whispered a prayer of thanks to the Lord Jesus. When she separated, Octavia's skin tingled from some unexplained sensation.

A throat cleared and Octavia turned in that direction. "Landon?" Her voice trembled as her vision blurred. "Why aren't you in Boston?"

It was as if everyone in the room held their breath as Octavia gasped for hers. Landon walked toward her. "I'm taking a later flight. Congratulations. This time I brought candy and flowers."

As Octavia's tears flowed, Landon made good on his promise. He tugged away from prying eyes and kissed her until she thought she would pass out.

27

The joy on Octavia's face, the kiss on her soft lips and her smile was worth Landon taking the last flight to Boston. Now stretching his legs in the window seat, Landon peeped out the window. He would be tired in the morning, but he was sure his children would keep him alert for an impromptu meet-and-greet at his parents' house.

Reba and Martin agreed to bring Alyssa. Surprisingly, Kim's agitation had been so intense as if they were face-to-face again.

"Yeah, I guess I'll bring Cherie, but you'd better not come to town without bringing cash."

Landon had held in his chuckle, so not to irritate an already volatile situation. "Right."

Kim would definitely be disappointed with a bank check this time since he had opened up a checking account. Plus, since graduating the father's initiative program, he had set up automatic deductions to come out of his bank three weeks a month, one for each set of his children. Thanks to Alyssa's stepfather's generosity, he would send his oldest daughter less, so he would have more to send the other three children.

He sighed when he thought about his twins and their mother.

For a woman who was engaged to a seemingly decent man who appeared to love her and the boys, Brittani proved to be just as difficult. He prayed God would deliver her of the hurts of the past, so she could move forward whenever they had to interact on behalf of the children.

Rest. Do not worry about tomorrow. God whispered Matthew 6:34. *Each day has its own trouble.*

Closing his eyes, Landon did just that, and he didn't stir until the attendant made an announcement to prepare for landing. Twenty minutes later when he walked off the plane, Landon felt the absence of his support team. The airport was deserted, except for passengers from his flight. This weekend would be about bonding.

Leaving the terminal for the baggage claim area, Landon did a double take. His eyes hadn't deceived him. A familiar face was standing near the window, holding a single balloon. Landon almost stumbled when their eyes connected.

"Garrett?" The man lived five hours away in Philly. Did he make a special trip to Boston to settle scores with him?

Wearing a blank expression, his cousin made no attempt to meet him halfway. As the only boys in their families and male grandsons, they were best buddies until they entered manhood. That's when Landon realized his light brown eyes, wavy hair and light skin had an edge with the ladies over Garrett. His cousin seemed to tolerate his shenanigans, but now things were different. Landon braced for an emergency room visit with a broken nose as he came within feet of the man he had betrayed.

"You're late." Garrett stated the obvious.

"I know."

As Garrett stared at him, Landon wondered what his cousin saw: the same sinner who mocked God repeatedly or a lost sheep that God had watched over until he surrendered.

Pushing away from the wall, which had supported his weight, Garrett stood taller. He had picked up some inches around the middle since his marriage to Shari, but it definitely wasn't fat. Slowly Garrett's hand moved and it wasn't in a fist as he extended it for a handshake. "Welcome home."

When Landon accepted the hand, Garrett wrapped him in a manly hug. To onlookers, there was no doubt they were one hundred percent all men.

Garrett patted him on the back as Landon choked back tears. "I'm so sorry I've messed over your life and others'. I'm sorry, man. I'm sorry."

His cousin squeezed his neck. Any tighter, it would have been unto death. "Aunt Lydia told me what you've been through. She, my mother and my wife thought it would be good for us to have a long talk."

Landon grinned. "I'll have to thank them."

"The good news is God got your attention before you were lost in eternity in hell. The bad news is you'll have to deal with Brittani for the rest of your life."

28

"I didn't threaten the man," Olivia insisted as she helped Octavia prepare a brunch Saturday morning for them to enjoy. "Landon and I just had a brief chat." Olivia gave her an angelic look. "If Daddy had come, Melvin Winston would have put the fear into Landon."

"Amen," she and Olivia snickered. Her father had been rooting for her since she began as a realtor. If he hadn't strained his back, he and his wife would have been on the next flight out of Florida. But Melvin Winston didn't let that setback stop him from having flowers delivered to her door this morning.

As daddy's little girl, Octavia wondered if Landon could have passed her father's scrutiny.

"But, hey, I like your taste," Olivia said, keeping her mind from wandering down that path. "Landon is double fine. Whew." Olivia feigned a hot flash, giggled, then set the counter top with two place settings.

Octavia held in her amusement. She didn't want to encourage her sister to intervene in her relationship with Landon.

As they worked in unison around her kitchen, Olivia chatted away. "I introduced myself and told him what it meant to have you as my sister...and how special you are from any other human being on this planet."

"Wow." The compliment humbled Octavia. "Thank you. I love you too." After removing the pancakes from the grill, she joined her sister at the tabletop.

"I mean, how can you threaten someone who already has experienced the hand of God against them?"

"You've got a point," Octavia paused and reached for her sister's hands, then bowed her head. "Jesus, I have so much to be thankful for, besides the food set before me—my sister and You giving me the desire of my heart," she said, convincing herself she was referring to making the Million Dollar Club. "Lord, please provide shelter and food for many faces I don't see who are hidden in plain sight and let be me a blessing to them." She paused. "Thank you for restoring Landon, and may he continue to mend the broken hearts. In Jesus' name. Amen."

After taking a sip of orange juice and sampling Octavia's made-from-scratch blueberry pancakes, Olivia asked, "What do you think he's doing now?"

"I hope having a ball with his children." It was a bittersweet smile. She wanted to have children one day with a husband who would be just as excited to be a first-time father. She blinked away the melancholy. Her sister was in town for the weekend and she was going to enjoy every minute of it.

"Really, Kim?" Landon tried not to let his daughter's mother push his buttons. "You knew I was coming in this weekend and my mother was having a get-together for me to get to know my children and their siblings." It wasn't like he could hop on a plane and come back to visit.

"Hey, I'm having car problems. If you want Cherie to go, then you'll have to come and get her." The woman hung up before Landon could blink.

Closing his eyes, Landon took a series of deep breaths and rubbed the back of his neck. "Lord, I know I have to reap what I've sowed, but I'm asking You to help me. In Jesus' name. Amen."

I have given you grace, the Lord whispered.

Landon hoped so as he opened his eyes. He noticed the time. He had a few hours before his other children would arrive. He was surprised that Kim trusted Cherie to be in his presence and thought she would want to be there to help with the transition, but he was starting to see that Kim, Reba and Brittani had different agendas with him.

Deal with it, Landon coaxed himself as he jumped in the shower. He would go and pick up his four-year-old daughter and be back before her siblings arrived.

His mother had suggested that a small gathering might be better rather than Landon allotting each child a certain amount of time. He agreed. His mother had decorated the house as if he was throwing a birthday bash for a classroom of children instead of four. Well, this was a celebration.

What a difference grace made. It seemed like yesterday when his mother had called him "devious" for fathering, not one or two, but four grandchildren she had yet to meet. Since that time, relationships had been built, but strained. Now, she received him with open arms and never used his deeds against him in a negative way.

The biggest surprise was his welcoming party of one at Logan airport the previous night. Landon hadn't expected to see Garrett ever again in this lifetime, but there he was at 11:43, standing in the lobby, holding a "welcome home" balloon.

"That was Shari's idea," Garrett had explained of the balloon before he dropped Landon off at his parents' house, then Garrett went to his mom and dad's where Shari and their children were staying. Garrett agreed to return with Shari and their two children to meet their cousins. Of course, his grandparents would not be denied an opportunity to bond with more of their great-grands. Moses and Queen were the first to arrive very early that morning to help.

With the new developments, Landon didn't have the luxury to continue analyzing how God had worked it out in his life. He prepared to get ready to pick up his little princess. Once he had shaved, showered, and dressed, Landon went downstairs and asked to borrow his mother's car.

"Son, you don't have to ask." She kissed his cheek. "Go and get my grand baby." She grinned and shoved him toward the door.

The drive to Northern Dorchester—shortened to "Dot" by Bostonians—wasn't far. Everything seemed surreal as he noted the different landmarks that separated familiar neighborhoods.

Soon enough, Landon was parked in front of Kim's place. She lived on the second floor of one of the triple-decker apartment buildings for which New England cities were known. He didn't get out right away as he mentally prepared to be a father to his own flesh and blood.

After a brief pep talk, Landon stepped out and jogged up the stairs. Kim didn't keep him waiting after he rang the bell. She opened the door with his daughter by her side and her palm up, waiting for her expected delivery. Once he handed over the envelope, she handed over the child as if they were doing a drug buy.

"Here, take this," she said, passing him what looked like a chair. "She needs a booster seat."

"Right." He nodded as he looked at Cherie's inquisitive brown eyes, which reminded him of Kim's. DNA testing proved the child was his in spite of his protests that they had only slept together a short period of time.

"Although you don't deserve seeing my daughter, this is an honor system. Don't call asking for her to spend the night, watch what she eats—she has no allergies—and bring her back before seven. "G'on, Cherie. This is your sorry father."

"Kim, let's make a deal," Landon said, reigning in his temper as she folded her arms and leaned against the door post. "You don't bad mouth me in front of *our* daughter, and I'll extend the

same courtesy. I plan to show her that her daddy is anything but
sorry." He fumed at Kim's lack of respect, but calmed down when
he reached for his daughter's hand. She was hesitant at first, but
after a few more tries, she accepted it. He heaved her up with one
arm as if she was a toddler instead of a four-year-old and carried
the booster in the other to the car. When he looked back, Kim had
already shut the door.

During the ride to his parents' house, Landon tried to make
small talk, but Cherie didn't seem interested as she alternated
between looking out the window and watching him. When he
arrived, Garrett and his crew were there. When everyone made a
fuss over his daughter, Landon's chest puffed with pride. He
stayed close to Cherie, so she wouldn't feel overwhelmed.

Within an hour, it was a madhouse as Brittani and Charles
arrived with the twins minutes after Reba and her husband had
brought Alyssa and decided to stay.

Garrett spoke to his ex-fiancée, but there weren't any hugs
coming. Landon was glad for Charles's presence, because he could
sense Brittani's troubled spirit. He hoped with Charles by her side,
Brittani wouldn't become a troublemaker.

The games and activities his mother had planned did the trick.
Soon the children were screaming, yelling and playing together.
Every now and then, Cherie peeked around searching for him, as if
making sure he hadn't left her. The contentment on her face made
him more determined to be there for his baby girl.

Landon could wait until the children had cake and ice cream,
then he would bring out the duffle bags he brought from St. Louis.
Rossi, Levi, his wife and Octavia had packed them almost to the
maximum weight with toys.

When the time came, he gathered all the children around and
began to dispense the many gifts he had brought from St. Louis.
The children screamed with delight at the toy trucks, Legos, dolls
and stuffed animals.

"I have plenty for my little cousins," he told Garrett when

Garrett's two sons got in line and expected a toy too. "Rossi and Octavia made sure of it."

Garrett gave him a strange look. "You mentioned her name last night—a couple of times—but I was too tired to ask about her. Aunt Lydia raved to Mom about how sweet and pretty she is, so..." Garrett nudged his shoulder.

He wasn't offended by what his cousin was implying. His grandfather was also concerned that Landon not stain Octavia with his sins. "If you're asking me if there is any lust in my bones toward her, the answer is no—I don't plan to sleep with another woman unless she's my wife."

"Good answer." Garrett nodded. "So, is she the one?"

"Yes...only if I have time to give her the attention she deserves." Landon never thought he would be in a position not to woo a woman, but he was now and he didn't know how to deal with it.

Garrett looked as if he was about to say something, but Landon cut him off when his eldest daughter, Alyssa, holding one of the African-American dolls that was in the toys he brought, gave him a hug and kiss on the cheek for no reason. "Wow," he whispered. Before he returned to St. Louis, his children would have him wrapped about their fingers.

Caught up in an awe moment, Landon didn't realize Garrett was grinning at him. "What, man? This is blowing my mind."

"Children will do that. Before your *daughter*—" Garrett emphasized the word— "interrupted us, and they do that all the time..." Garrett's oldest son appeared as if to prove it.

Landon watched as Garrett patiently showed Garrison how to operate the game, then the boy went back to play with the others. He snickered and turned his attention back to Landon. "Explain to me how a woman could be 'the one' and you not go after her?"

The room reminded him of Christmas with all the toys and discarded wrappings. He fanned his hand in the air. "Look around you. Most of the children here are mine. Not one child and one child's mother to deal with, but four children and three mothers. What woman would want to be a part of this kind of drama?"

"Maybe, you should ask her and find out, because it sounds like she is the one that you're about to let get away." Garrett got to his feet when he saw that his son had pushed his little brother out the way. "Just remember, Octavia has seen you at your worse—no home, job and food and she's still there. Sounds like a strong black godly woman and that is something every black man needs. I've got mine and God knows, she's not going anywhere until He calls her home."

Landon exhaled. Garrett was right. Landon couldn't let Octavia get away, especially to the likes of characters like James. Although family and his children surrounded him, Landon felt incomplete without Octavia sharing in this moment with him. After a few minutes of thinking things through, Landon came to a decision. If he could be a father of four, then he could be a husband to one woman.

29

Late Sunday night, Landon boarded the plane at Logan Airport, feeling like…a dad. The gathering had given him insight to each of his children's unique personality. Alyssa had created a lasting memory. His little girl had asked Reba and her stepdad if she could go to the airport to see her "extra" daddy—as she had called him a couple of times at the party—home.

Strapped in his seatbelt, Landon closed his eyes. He never had felt so loved and sad to leave. If left up to him, Landon would move back to Boston in a heartbeat. As his plane soared into the sky, his thoughts changed to what was awaiting him in St. Louis.

Octavia. He wanted her, and whatever he had to do or say to make it permanent, he was willing to do it. After all, wouldn't his children want him to be happy?

The pilot touched down in St. Louis exactly two hours later—a smooth ride with no delays. He mingled with the other travelers as they exited the terminal.

His nostrils flared at the sight of Octavia. Had she come to the airport to welcome him? That was so much like her, he thought, but as he walked closer, Landon saw her waving goodbye to her sister. The joke was on him. Her life didn't revolve around him.

Olivia was sweet, but Octavia definitely was the beauty. Walking quietly behind her, Landon whispered in her ear, "Hello, pretty lady."

She whirled around as he opened his arms. When she flew into them, he kissed her, then squeezed her close. She tried to pull away, but he wouldn't let her. Only when he needed to breathe did he loosen his hold, but not his contact as he wrapped his arm around her waist and steered her toward baggage claim with him.

She smiled and squeezed his waist. "So how was daddy duty?"

"Uh-uh." He shook his head. "I want to talk about us. Timing is everything. I'm glad you were here, even if it was to see Olivia off. I've made some decisions, and I want to talk to you about them."

"Tonight?" She cast him a suspicious look.

"Tomorrow," he stated and guided her downstairs where his bag was spinning on the carousel. He linked his fingers through hers as he reached down and retrieved it.

"Since I'm here, I can give you a ride home," she offered.

"It's late and I'm out of your way. I'll catch the Metrolink and then the bus." When it appeared she was about to protest, he kissed her. "Baby, don't argue with me," he whispered against her lips. He proceeded to escort her to her car, then he waited until she was off. Twirling around, he jogged up the stairs to the Metrolink train platform. He smiled to himself as he took a seat. "Nope, I'm not going to let another man have you."

Don't think I didn't see that! Sweet dreams.

Octavia read her sister's text the next morning and grinned. After returning from the airport the night before, Landon had given her something sweet to dream about. The look in his eyes and the kiss on her lips made it impossible not to. As she sauntered into the office for the Monday morning meeting, her colleagues thought her glow came from her recent milestone.

"A million dollars didn't buy that glow. Hmm-mm," Terri teased and lifted her brow.

"You know money can't buy you happiness," Octavia said in a sing-song tone and put away her purse to prepare for the meeting. Terri went through her spiel and advised her agents of new listings. When the meeting concluded, Octavia thought about Landon and wondered how he was doing on his first day of regular employment. She prayed God's continued favor over his life.

A few hours later, Octavia was following up on leads when she felt a presence. Looking up from her desk, Octavia blinked as "wow" echoed around in her mouth before it escaped and vibrated through the air. She had seen Landon in a shirt and tie when he worked at Rossi's, but the man before her was wearing a suit. If it weren't tailor made, it was a close fit. "What are you doing here?"

"Can I take you to lunch?" His eyes sparkled.

"Yes."

Gathering her purse, she waved at Terri. Once they were outside, she saw Rossi's company car and questioned him.

Landon shrugged. "He thought I should drive to the new job the first week. After that, I'll bus it until I can save for a car." Helping her inside, he drove the short distant to a picnic area near the zoo in Forest Park. They settled on a bench at a table and he gave her one of the foam containers that held their lunch.

"So how is your first day?" Octavia was excited for him and eager to hear the details.

"You know how it is to be the new kid on the block—new faces and names. People knew of me from my contributions on some outsourced campaigns."

He grinned. "We're in a tech-savvy world with tech issues. My boss told me to take a couple of hours for lunch while they work on resolving them." He paused. "I couldn't think of any other person I would rather spend my lunch with."

Lowering her eyes, she blushed. "That's sweet."

He gently engulfed her hands in his, then bowed his head to

say grace. "Jesus, I didn't realize I could love You as much as I do at this moment, because truly you have blessed me. Thank you for the love of a good woman, even if she has never said it…"

Octavia sucked in her breath.

"Lord, I see that my life is bigger than me and that everything I have is because You gave it to me…Please bless and sanctify our lives as You do this food and remove all impurities from our lives and in this food. In Jesus' name. Amen."

As Octavia listened to his prayer, she teared at his earnest petition before God. She quickly covered her face with her hands or Landon would make good on his threat to kiss her if she cried. No, she wanted to cherish this moment together and linger in the spiritual realm.

Taking a deep breath, she stood and put distance between them. She needed a praise moment to speak with God and worship Him for Landon's redemption. As she prayed, God communicated with her through heavenly tongues, and soon, she felt Landon's presence. It was surreal as they continued to pray and worship God together.

Once they were composed, Landon guided her back to her table. Before they even touched their food, he got on one knee.

"Octavia, I have only my love and faithfulness at this time. My pockets aren't filled with money and I'm eying an old clunker to get around in, yet with everything within me, I want you. Marry me and be the mother of my children."

As she looked into his not-quite hazel-colored eyes, she felt each sincere declaration. It was clear that he loved her. The confusion came when he said, "mother of my children." That could be interpreted so many ways, but she didn't ask him to break it down.

"I've lost everything to find you." He used his thumb to wipe at her eyes. "I believe God had this appointed time for our paths to cross. Otherwise, I might have hurt you and I repent even at that thought."

She reached out and massaged his smooth jaw. A light breeze circled around them and stirred his cologne, which she inhaled deeply. She remained speechless as he poured out his soul.

"When I was in Boston, I thought I had a readymade family, but my cousin, Garrett—praise God, he forgave me—reminded me that I'm a readymade father. Can you hang in there with me and be a stepmother to my children and a wife to me?"

His puppy dog eyes tugged at her heart, but she had to be frank now that it was her turn to speak. "No and yes."

Landon's eyes widened. "Huh?"

Pulling his face closer to hers, Octavia wanted to make sure he understood her position. "I don't know how to be a stepmother, and I don't want to learn. I'd love to be a mother to your children and ours, then yes…" Before Octavia could blink, Landon leaped up and took her with him. He hugged her as if she was a lifeline. "I'll marry you," she was able to finish through their moment of celebration.

Taking a seat on the bench again, Landon pulled her close. He hugged her; peppered kisses on her cheeks, mouth and hair; then hugged her again. "I can't afford a ring until the end of the month. My children wiped me out." He grinned.

Marry this man, and you'll struggle from day one. The thought came from nowhere and it frightened her.

Without knowing it, she had taken the devil's bait as all the excitement seemed to seep out of her. "Can you afford me?" She patted her chest. "A wife?"

He gave her the oddest expression before answering. "Although it may take a while before I bounce back financially, you will never go hungry. It may not be at a five-star restaurant, but you'll never go without. I asked you to marry me because I couldn't wait any longer. I've figured out my priorities. You'll always come first—always, until death we do part."

"I believe you." She smiled then reached for the deli sandwich he'd brought her. Their emotional charge had left her hungry. Before her first bite, she had a message for the devil. *Satan, I rebuke you! My marriage will work.*

30

"What was I thinking?" Landon shook his head until his eyes fluttered open. Landon groaned as if he was coming out of a morning hangover. He should have never proposed to Octavia. He wasn't ready.

"I don't know, man, but you were sure mumbling in your sleep about it," Grady said, startling Landon. Sometimes he forgot he had a roommate.

Pulling back his covers, Grady stared at Landon. "Do you want to talk about it, because when I move at the end of the month, you might not have a roomie cool like me?" He displayed a boyish grin.

"I'm right behind you in another month." Landon sat up and threw a pillow at Grady.

When Landon first arrived at Mac's Place, he wasn't too keen on sharing a room, and to top it off, with a young man who was reading his Bible. But God... He had strategically placed people in his life for his own good. Since his turnaround, he and Grady had bonded over the Bible.

"Just don't forget about us little people."

"Never again." Landon stood, slapped Grady's hand for a

shake, then gathered his things for a shower. "Oh, and I'll make sure you get an invite to the wedding," he said casually as he walked out the door. Grinning, he counted as he waited for the news to sink in.

"What?" Grady jumped to his feet, then pumped his hand. "Oh, no, you're getting cold feet already?" He bowed over laughing.

Shaking his head, Landon said, "No regrets on asking, only how I did it. It was on impulse—no ring—at a picnic bench." He cringed. "It was a sorry excuse for a proposal. I should have had a ring and made it special because she's special," he chided himself as he continued on to the showers.

Landon made a resolve. He didn't care if he had to work three jobs and postpone a trip to Boston. He was determined to go over the top to pamper Octavia with what she deserved. The standoff with James flashed in his mind as he scrubbed. Landon snarled thinking about it. He would make sure that Octavia would never regret choosing him over that dude.

Two weeks and counting. Octavia frowned. She had been an engaged woman for fourteen days, and since then her fiancé had been a no-show. Well, not exactly a no-show, but working. To make up for his absence, he sent her texts, which made her heart flutter. Sometimes the weekends were all they had, and even that was limited because of house showings. Not this weekend, Octavia thought, smiling. They had cleared Friday evening for dinner and Saturday morning for bunch. She couldn't wait.

Octavia had been home barely an hour when he called. "Hey, babe.' Landon sounded exhausted. "I love you."

"I love you and I miss you, too," she cooed as she searched her closet for something to wear.

"You have no idea how much…" He paused. "I'm really sorry, but can you hold all that love you have for me until tomorrow?

When I see you, I want to look presentable and right, not like I'm broke-down tired."

Her heart sunk in disappointment. Tonight was supposed to be the highlight of her day, but she couldn't fault Landon for working hard at two jobs. His pride this time was misplaced. She offered to pick him up, but Landon would rather catch the bus and have her meet him places than have her pick him up from Mac's Place. He said it was a man thing, so she respected his wish.

"Okay. I'm going to get some rest, and I'll see you in the morning."

"Wait!" Octavia yelled. "Where?"

"See you tomorrow." *Click.*

Placing her black dress back on the hanger, Octavia stepped out of the closet and took a cleansing breath. She was tired, too, but the thought of seeing Landon gave her energy. She headed toward her kitchen for a snack before going to bed. Now Saturday morning would have to be the highlight of her day.

The next morning, Octavia was dressed by ninety-thirty. She wore fall shades of brown and green. She always received compliments on any shades of red, but rust seemed to accent her unusual blondish-brown hair. She admired her flirty appearance and hoped Landon would too, if he would only call or text her back. She had no idea where to meet him. Finally, at five minutes before ten, he sent her a text. *Open the door and follow the path.*

Huh? Her subdivision wasn't on a bus route. Peeping outside her front window, there was indeed a trail of red roses that began at her front door. She frowned as she grabbed her keys and locked her door. It was unusual to see many of her neighbors standing on their porches this early and looking toward her house as if they had a heads-up on something. Some were grinning, others waving— she even got a couple thumbs-ups. The cool October morning was a welcome respite from the lingering summer heat, but there was a slight chill, and she thought about going back inside for a sweater, but curiosity had her follow the path until she turned the corner, and that's when she froze and gasped.

Her eyes blurred at the sight of the longest stretch Hummer limo she had ever seen. There was a photographer and another with a video camera pointing in her direction. The door opened, and Landon stepped out dressed in a tuxedo. Her mouth dropped. He was a prince magnified. In synchronized actions, he knelt as he opened his hand to display a ring box. A gentle wind seemed to nudge her forward until she towered over him. "You already proposed to me," she said in awe. It was nothing on this scale, but it was her moment to cherish forever.

"But not the right way, baby." He shook his head. "You're a jewel, and I promise you, I'll treat you as my queen until the day I die."

As if cued, four women spilled out of the limo and fitted her head with a tiara, then wrapped a silk shawl the same color green as her skirt, as if he knew her wardrobe, around her shoulders. She remembered him asking her long ago about her favorite colors. *Landon remembered.* His baritone voice began the words to "My Destiny" as the ladies backed him with up the chorus. The dam of her emotions spilled, and she cried unchecked as Landon stood, pulled her closer, then slipped a beautiful ring on her finger. She didn't care if there weren't any diamonds, she thought until something winked at her. There was at least one.

Instead of kissing her, Landon wiped at her tears as he continued to serenade her. The moment was surreal as her neighbors crowded around them.

Octavia's head was spinning by the time Landon finished the last note solo. She opened her mouth, but words couldn't describe what she was feeling. As Landon waited for her response, she placed her hands on the side of his face and whispered her love before she sealed it with a kiss.

Her stomach growled, killing the moment. She blushed and looked away. "You did promise me breakfast, and I haven't eaten."

That seemed to cue two servers to step out of the limo. "What else is in there, a house?" She walked closer to peep inside to find—her dad and his wife? Olivia was inside along with Rossi, his cousin and wife and Terri sitting at small makeshift tables.

"Congratulations," they screamed as if she hadn't already been engaged for almost a month.

Landon helped her inside and took the seat next to her.

"This is so romantic," Octavia lowered her voice. "But this cost a lot of money. How did you pay for all this?"

Placing his arm around her shoulder, he grinned. "I'm an account rep, babe. When I mentioned to my client Dingo Limo Service that I wanted to impress my fiancée with a proper proposal, they offered their services and asked if it could be taped for a commercial, so we had our moment on our own reality show. Another client offered the tux."

"And the ring?"

"That I worked every muscle in my body to buy." He looked into her eyes.

"Please let your clients know I was wowed," she said.

He winked, then smirked. "I think as soon as they see the video, they'll know."

Suddenly, she playfully punched him in the arm. "Why didn't you tell me you could sing like that?"

"I once was a choir boy, remember?" He chuckled.

So with all her questions answered, Octavia cuddled closer as two waiters served them fruit, juice and mini waffles. She never would have thought a man with so little could give her so much. Landon Thomas was rich in his love

31

A month later, Octavia accompanied Landon on a weekend trip to Boston. Olivia tagged along to act as their chaperon to enforce the "let your good be not evil spoken of" clause when it came to dating and a Christian woman's reputation. Once their plane landed, the Miller and Thomas families enforced their own rules with bedroom assignments at his grandfather's house instead of at the hotel where Landon had originally booked their stay.

His grandparents entertained her and Olivia with stories and baby pictures and so much food. It was a relaxing night, which Octavia appreciated because she didn't know what the next day would bring.

Saturday morning, Octavia woke to the aroma of biscuits, eggs and sausage. She and Olivia quickly showered and dressed and then greeted everyone in the kitchen as Landon was coming through the door with a single flower.

His demonstration of love received *oohs* and *ahhs* from his family. Once everyone had stuffed themselves, Landon was ready to see his children. Octavia did her best not to display her apprehension about seeing Landon's exes again.

Their first stop was at the Kees: Reba, Martin and Alyssa. His daughter was glad to see him as she hugged and kissed him.

"You remember, Miss Octavia," he asked Alyssa. "Well, I'm going to marry her," Landon said with pride and love in his eyes. The child's parents clapped and offered congratulations. "Are you going to be my extra mommy?" Alyssa asked her.

Huh? Stepmother she expected, but extra mommy? Once Landon explained to her where the term originated from, she smiled. "Yes, I will."

That earned Octavia a hug. "If it's okay with you—" she glanced at Reba—"we would love for her to be in our wedding. You and your husband are invited to come as well."

Alyssa grinned and jumped on one foot. "Can I, Mommy?"

"Of course," her parents answered in unison.

The child gave her and Landon a group hug and kiss.

Octavia enjoyed the visit and the pleasant conversation. She felt relaxed and encouraged that Reba would guide her in her parenting skills with Alyssa. When she, Olivia and Landon left, mother and daughter seemed disappointed.

The next couple of stops proved to be more challenging. Unlike her first visit, Landon's other daughter, Cherie, greeted him with a hug with little coaxing. Not only was she a little suspect of Octavia, but so was her mother—the same woman who refused her in her house the first time.

"Is that the crazy one?" Olivia asked under her breath.

Octavia nudged her to be discreet. "There's one crazier than her," she mumbled. "So let's pray." And all three did as they entered Kim's house. Octavia could feel the presence of demonic influences around them.

Octavia called on the name of Jesus so the demons would tremble and flee. While Landon was distracted with Cherie, Octavia tried to get to know the child's mother. It didn't help that Landon introduced her as his fiancée, which seemed to put Kim on the defense.

"This is a nice place," Octavia complimented as she scanned

the living room and the other she could see.

Kim shrugged. "It'll do. It's the best my money can buy. Maybe, now that Landon is paying his share again, Cherie and I might move."

Octavia tried to engage Kim in movies, hobbies, fashion, but the woman's one word and brief answers suggested she didn't want to be bothered. Octavia watched as Landon said his goodbye to Cherie at least three times. It was apparent he didn't want to leave. At the door, Landon gave Cherie one more kiss and faced her mother. "I would like for my daughter to be in my wedding.

"Humph, I'm not coming to St. Louis," Kim snapped.

"I'll come and get Cherie," Landon said in an even tone as if he were trying to hold it together. Octavia didn't know if she should reach for his hand as a sign of moral support, or if the gesture would set Kim off, so she and Olivia remained quiet and praying.

"You pay for everything, and I'll think about it."

After saying their goodbyes, Octavia listened to Landon's heavy footsteps from the door to the car. She exchanged glances with Olivia before reading Landon's body language—he was tense. After they were strapped in and ready to drive away, Landon took a deep breath before starting the ignition. "That woman is going..." He gritted his teeth. "She's going to push the wrong button, and I'll—"

"And you'll what?" she said softly. Octavia reached over and linked her fingers through his. "Cherie's mother will be in our lives permanently. You and I will pray that God will intervene and soften her heart. It might take a while or it may come instantly, but we're a praying team."

"You're right, babe." He glanced at her, then squeezed her hand before bringing it to his lips where his mustache tickled her skin.

She spoke positive words and quoted a few scripture verses to comfort his spirit. Soon, he shared some of the funny things Cherie asked him. The mood was jovial as they parked in front of the last residence about thirty minutes later. After this stop, he promised to take her and Olivia sightseeing. What a difference a trip made.

"Yay, yay," Olivia said as if she was a kid herself.

It was déjà vu for Octavia when Brittani opened the door. The woman still wore the same attitude, but on a different day. Octavia summed her up in one word: bitter. The boys, on the other hand, weren't shy about seeing their father and were ready to go outside and play, so that's what they did as she, Olivia and Brittani stood on the porch and watched for about twenty minutes or so. Brittani wasn't pleased that Octavia was engaged to Landon and she wasn't happy that Octavia had brought her sister. Brittani was just plain "not happy."

Brittani wore an engagement ring, but that didn't seem to keep the contempt from her eyes. "Landon, do you mind if we speak in private?" she asked.

Not only did Landon seem annoyed by the interruption, but the twins made their displeasure known.

"We can watch the boys," Octavia offered.

"You do that." Brittani jutted her chin and went inside the house as Landon followed. Octavia learned "private" to Brittani meant "behind her back instead of in front of her face" as her voice was anything but a hush. "She'd better not mistreat my boys when they come to visit."

"Both crazies are tied in first place," Olivia mouth and giggled.

"Watch it, Brittani," She overheard Landon say in a low, but stern voice. "For the sake of our sons, I want us to have a working relationship, but we'd better set the ground rules now. Octavia doesn't deserve your meanness. If you would take the time to get to know her, I think you'd like her, but I don't care, because I love her. Don't you ever—I mean ever—disrespect us again. Did I say ever?"

"And what are you going to do about it?" she sassed him.

"Trust me, you don't want to find out…" Landon walked out of the house. He smiled at Octavia, then urged the boys to play another round of catch as if he hadn't spoken a cross word minutes earlier. This time, Brittani stayed inside.

Octavia relaxed, but she knew her marriage to Landon would include a lot of prayer and fasting for the sake of tranquility for the children. As she watched father and sons horseplay, Octavia wondered in Landon's case, who had been the seducer and prey. Landon thought it was him, but maybe he had been Brittani's prey all along, and it would bruise Landon's ego to point out how he had been used. She snickered at the probability, but he would never, ever, ever hear that from her.

Soon it was time to go, and they were back in the car. Landon was out of breath, but he was glowing with happiness. Watching him interact with the children, a thought came to Octavia. She lowered her voice so Olivia couldn't hear. "Babe, have you considered moving back to Boston, so you can be closer to the children? It definitely would be cheaper, and I'm…okay with that."

Landon stared at her. The love shone from his eyes. "As a matter of fact, I have. I thought about it long and hard, and prayed for direction. God spoke to me and told me if I take you as my wife, you would be my priority." He leaned over and brushed the softest kiss against her lips. "Thank you, baby, for offering." Before pulling back, Landon pecked a few more kisses on her lips, then mumbled, "Come on June 24th."

Octavia smiled. Yes, their wedding couldn't come soon enough.

"Excuse me, there's a child in the car," Olivia said from the back seat, and they all burst out laughing.

32

Six months later, on the third Sunday in June, Landon stood in Forest Park under a brass arch that had been intertwined with flowers. The day was extra special because it was the first time he would celebrate Father's Day with all four of his children.

Octavia had planned the day to perfection. Benson and Bryan were ring bearers while his daughters shared the spotlight as the flower girls.

As he waited for his bride, Landon glanced around at the guests who had sacrificed their Father's Day to be there for him: cousins—even Garrett and his wife—uncles, aunts, his grandparents, old friends and new.

His musings were dashed at the first chord of the "Wedding March" when Octavia appeared. When his jaw dropped, Garrett, a groomsman, nudged him. "Close it before something flies in."

Rossi, his other groomsman, and his father, who was the best man, chuckled.

But Landon did as instructed. The only thing he wanted to taste was his wife's lips. His heart thundered against his chest in excitement. Instead of Octavia getting lost in yards of fabric, she was stunning in a sleek fabric that draped her figure, but still left a lot to his imagination. She had that wow factor on him every time he looked at her.

God, what did I do to deserve her? he thought.

Absolutely nothing, God whispered back and Landon smiled.

A slight breeze ushered her closer. Landon stepped from his post to meet her. He shook hands with her father.

The music continued to play, but Landon didn't budge. This was his day—their day—and he wanted to catalog everything. Octavia's curls were glossy and styled to frame her gorgeous face. "Thank You, Jesus," he said and exhaled. Octavia Winston was about to be Octavia Thomas within minutes.

"Landon, babe," she whispered, "You're supposed to walk me to the altar."

He bit his bottom lip and nodded. "Right." Landon lingered a moment longer then escorted her until they were standing in front of his former pastor from his home church in Boston who had volunteered to officiate.

"It would be my honor to be part of your restoration. Your marriage will be a testament to God's salvation that you're an overcomer," Pastor Justice had said when Landon spoke to him in confidence when he was in Boston on his last trip.

"Dearly beloved, we are gathered here today to celebrate the union of Brother Landon Thomas and Sister Octavia Winston…"

The couple barely made it through their vows as Landon tried his best to hold back tears and Octavia's flowed freely while her sister dabbed at her cheeks.

"You promise before God's presence that you will forsake all others. Let no man or woman come between you, be loyal and loving at all times…" He looked at Landon. "Cherish her at all times. Never forget the priceless jewel you have."

"Never—ever," he whispered.

Then the pastor turned to Octavia. "Respect him, submit to him, hold him up before God and most importantly love him. By the power vested in me, I now pronounce you husband and wife.

What God has joined together, let no woman, man, or child come between you in the name of our Lord and Savior Jesus Christ. Amen." He paused. "Brother Landon, you may now salute your—"

"Daddy, I've got to pee," Benson said, shattering the moment as Landon glanced down at his son who was holding his pants.

"Not now, son," Landon hushed.

"I'll take him," his grandfather volunteered as everyone chuckled.

"Without further delay, you may kiss your bride." Pastor Justice smiled.

Sweeping Octavia into his arms, he kissed her and then placed pecks on her cheeks until he whispered into her ear, "I'll never make you regret being my wife."

"I know." They kissed again, and the rest was history.

EPILOGUE

O*ne year later...*

Octavia Thomas massaged her husband's shoulders as he poured over contracts he needed to sign to start his own small business marketing firm. He already had three clients waiting to come on board.

She was so proud of Landon. He was an outstanding ad rep, an attentive husband and a dedicated father.

She couldn't ask for a better mate. Octavia doubted he would be the man he was without being tried through the fire of his trials. "How's it going?"

He glanced over his shoulder and coaxed her closer for a kiss. "I believe God will bless us." He winked. "I've got one more year to show the bankruptcy court that I'm credit worthy again and then I'm buying *us* our first house."

"You know that's not necessary. You insist on paying the mortgage here, and your name was added to the deed."

"But *I* didn't buy it for *you*. I plan to change that." Shoving the files aside, Landon stood and snaked his arms around her waist, pulling her closer. "Besides, we're going to need a bigger house as our family grows."

She laughed as Landon lovingly rubbed her stomach. At four months, Octavia had a bump. She couldn't wait to cradle a new baby in her arms. As Landon's smaller children had gotten in a habit of calling her an extra mommy from Alyssa, they all couldn't wait to have an extra brother or sister.

She and Landon still hadn't ruled out a permanent move to the New England state, but as Landon assured her, "The children will grow up and leave home, but you...I'll have you as long as the Lord gives us breath."

"In Jesus' name, I receive that. Amen." She squeezed his neck.

"You know what? I think you need to take a nap, and I think I'll join you," he said with a naughty grin before scooping her up and carrying her into their bedroom. When the door closed, they shut out the world. And the honeymoon continued.

BOOK CLUB DISCUSSIONS:

1. Landon was reared in the church and knew better than to dishonor God. Talk about the consequences of a lukewarm person's actions.

2. Octavia made a choice to love Landon. Why?

3. Landon had fathered four children. Discuss his revelation of what it took to be a daddy.

4. Landon was portrayed as characters from the Bible: Jacob and Esau; the prodigal son and the lost sheep. Which scenario do you think he identified with most in the story?

5. Discuss Octavia's relationship with Terri in regards to Terri pushing Octavia toward James.

6. What lesson did you receive from this story?

7. Based on Landon's past transgressions, how easy would it be for you to forgive someone like him?

A SPECIAL THANK YOU.

I'm honored that you chose *Redeeming Heart* to read. I not only hope you have enjoyed Landon and Octavia's story, but you were blessed.

Please consider posting an honest review on Amazon, so others will know what you thought about this story.

If you're interested in being part of my street team to help me get the word out about my Christian titles, please email me at authorpatsimmons@gmail.com.

Most of all, may God bless you for blessing me!

Pat Simmons

ABOUT THE AUTHOR

Pat is the multi-published author of several single titles and eBook novellas, and is a two-time recipient of the Emma Rodgers Award for Best Inspirational Romance. She has been a featured speaker and workshop presenter at various venues across the country.

As a self-proclaimed genealogy sleuth, Pat is passionate about researching her ancestors and then casting them in starring roles in her novels. She describes the evidence of the gift of the Holy Ghost as an amazing, unforgettable, life-altering experience. God is the Author who advances the stories she writes.

Pat is currently overseeing the media publicity for the annual RT Booklovers Conventions. She has a B.S. in mass communications from Emerson College in Boston, Massachusetts.

Pat converted her sofa-strapped, sports fanatic husband into an amateur travel agent, untrained bodyguard, GPS-guided chauffeur, and administrative assistant who is constantly on probation. They have a son and a daughter.

Read more about Pat and her books by visiting www.patsimmons.net or on social media.

OTHER CHRISTIAN TITLES BY PAT SIMMONS INCLUDE:

The Guilty series
Book I: *Guilty of Love*
Book II: *Not Guilty of Love*
Book III: *Still Guilty*

The Guilty Parties series
Book I: *The Acquittal*
Book II: *The Confession*

The Jamieson Legacy
Book I: *Guilty by Association*
Book II: *The Guilt Trip*
Book III: *Free from Guilt*

The Carmen Sisters
Book I: *No Easy Catch*
Book II: *In Defense of Love*
Redeeming Heart
Book III: *Driven to Be Loved*

Love at the Crossroads
Book I: *Stopping Traffic*
Book II: *A Baby for Christmas*

Book III: *The Keepsake*
Book IV: *What God Has for Me*

Making Love Work Anthology
Book I: *Love at Work*
Book II: *Words of Love*
Book III: *A Mother's Love*

Single titles
Crowning Glory
Talk to Me
Her Dress (novella)

Holiday titles
Love for the Holidays
(Three Christian novellas)
A Christian Christmas
A Christian Easter
A Christian Father's Day
A Woman After David's Heart (Valentine's Day)
Christmas Greetings

LOVE AT THE CROSSROADS SERIES

—STOPPING TRAFFIC—

Candace Clark has a phobia about crossing the street. As fate would have it, her daughter's principal assigns her to crossing guard duties as part of the school's parent participation program. Candace begrudgingly accepts her stop sign and safety vest, then reports to her designated crosswalk. She's determined to overcome her fears, and God opens the door for a blessing, and Royce Kavanaugh enters into her life, a firefighter built to rescue any damsel in distress.

—A BABY FOR CHRISTMAS—

Yes, diamonds are a girl's best friend, but in Solae Wyatt-Palmer's case, she desires something more valuable. Captain Hershel Kavanaugh is a divorcee and the father of two adorable little boys. Solae has never been married and longs to be a mother. Although Hershel showers her with expensive gifts, his hesitation about proposing causes Solae to walk and never look back. As the holidays approach, Hershel must convince Solae that she has everything he could ever want for Christmas.

—THE KEEPSAKE—

Until death us do part... Desiree "Desi" Bishop is devastated when she learns of her husband's affair. God knew she didn't get married only to one day have to stand before a judge and file for a divorce. But Desi wants out no matter how much her heart says to forgive Michael. She sees God's one acceptable reason for a divorce as the only opt-out clause in her marriage. Michael Bishop is a repenting man who loves his wife. If only...he had paid attention to the red flags God sent to keep him from falling into the devil's snares. Although God's forgives instantly, Desi's forgiveness is moving as a snail's pace. After all the tears have been shed and forgiveness granted and received, the couple learns that some marriages are worth keeping.

—WHAT GOD HAS FOR ME—

Pregnant Halcyon Holland is leaving her live-in boyfriend, taking their daughter with her. When her ex doesn't reconcile their relationship, Halcyon begins to second-guess whether or not she compromised her chance for a happily ever after. But Zachary Bishop has had his eye on Halcyon for a long time. Without a ring on her finger, Zachary prays that she will come to her senses and not only leave Scott, but come back to God. What one man doesn't cherish, Zach is ready to treasure. Not deterred by Halcyon's broken spirit, Zachary is on a mission to offer her a second chance at love that she can't refuse. And as far as her adorable children are concerned, Zachary's love is unconditional for a ready-made family. Halcyon will soon learn that her past circumstances won't hinder the Lord's blessings, because what God has for her, is for her

LOVE FOR THE HOLIDAYS SERIES

—A CHRISTIAN CHRISTMAS—

Christmas will never be the same for Joy Knight if Christian Andersen has his way. Christian and his family are busy making sure the Lord's blessings are distributed to those less fortunate by Christmas day. Joy is playing the hand that life dealt her, rearing four children in a home that is on the brink of foreclosure. She's not looking for a handout when Christian Andersen rescues her in the checkout line. Can time spent with him turn Joy's attention from her financial woes to the real meaning of Christmas and true love?

—A CHRISTIAN EASTER—

How to celebrate Easter becomes a balancing act for Christian and Joy Andersen and their four children. Chocolate bunnies, colorful stuffed baskets and flashy fashion shows are their competition. Despite the enticements, Christian refuses to succumb without a fight. And it becomes a tug of war when his recently adopted ten year-old daughter, Bethani, wants to participate in her friend's Easter tradition. Christian hopes he has instilled Proverbs 22:6, into the children's heart in the short time of being their dad.

—A CHRISTIAN FATHER'S DAY—

Three fathers, one Father's Day and four children. Will the real dad, please stand up. It's never too late to be a father—or is it? Christian Andersen was looking forward to spending his first Father's day with his adopted children—all four of them. But Father's day becomes more complicated than Christian or Joy ever imagined. Christian finds himself faced with living up to his name when things don't go his way to enjoy an idyllic once a year celebration. But he depends on God to guide him through the journey.

—A WOMAN AFTER DAVID'S HEART—

David Andersen doesn't want a woman to get any ideas that a wedding ring was forthcoming before he got a chance to know her if their first date is on Valentine's Day. So he has no choice but to wait until the whole Valentine's Day hoopla was over, then he would make his move on a sister in his church he can't take his eyes off of. For the past two years and counting, Valerie Hart hasn't been the recipient of a romantic Valentine's Day dinner invitation. To fill the void, Valerie keeps herself busy with God's business, hoping the Lord will send her perfect mate soon.

—CHRISTMAS GREETINGS—

For Saige Carter, Christmas wouldn't be complete without family and friends to share in the traditions they've created together. Plus, Saige is extra excited about her line of Christmas greeting cards hitting store shelves, but when she gets devastating news around the holidays, she wonders if she'll ever look at Christmas the same again.

Daniel Washington is no Scrooge, but he'd rather skip the holidays altogether than spend them with his estranged family. After one too many arguments around the dinner table one year, Daniel had enough and walked away from the drama. When Daniel reads one of Saige's greeting cards, he's unsure if the words inside are enough to erase the pain and bring about forgiveness.

MAKING LOVE WORK SERIES

—A MOTHER'S LOVE—

Jillian Carter became a teenage mother when she confused love for lust one summer. Despite the sins of her past, Jesus forgave her and blessed her to be the best Christian example for Shana. Jillian is not looking forward to becoming an empty-nester at thirty-nine. The old adage, she's not losing a daughter, but gaining a son-in-law is not comforting as she braces for a lonely life ahead. Shana's biological father breezes back into their lives as a redeemed man and practicing Christian. Not only is Alex still good-looking, but he's willing to right the wrong he's done in the past. The widower father of the groom, Dr. Dexter Harris, has set his sights on Jillian and he's willing to pull out all the stops to woo her. Now the choice is hers. Who will be the next mother's love?

—LOVE AT WORK—

How do two people go undercover to hide an office romance in a busy television newsroom? In plain sight, of course. Desiree King is an assignment editor at KDPX-TV in St. Louis, MO. She dispatches a team to wherever breaking news happens. When it comes to dating a fellow coworker, she refuses to cross that professional line. Award-winning investigative reporter Brooke Mitchell makes life challenging for

Desiree with his thoughtful gestures, sweet notes, and support. He tries to convince Desiree that as Christians, they could show coworkers how to blend their personal and private lives without compromising their morals.

—WORDS OF LOVE—

Simone French was smitten with a love letter. Not a text, email, or Facebook post, but a love letter sent through snail mail. The prose wasn't the corny roses-are-red-and-violets-are-blue stuff. The first letter contained short accolades for a job well done. Soon after, the missives were filled with passionate words from a man who confessed the hidden secrets of his soul. He revealed his unspoken weaknesses, listed his uncompromising desires, and unapologetically noted his subtle strengths. Yes, Rice Taylor was ready to surrender to love. Whew. Closing her eyes, Simone inhaled the faint lingering smell of roses on the beige plain stationery. She had a testimony. If anyone would listen, she would proclaim that love was truly blind.

—MY TESTIMONY: IF I SHOULD DIE BEFORE I WAKE—

It is of the LORD's mercies that we are not consumed, because His compassions fail not. They are new every morning, great is Thy faithfulness. Lamentations 3:22-23, God's mercies are sure; His promises are fulfilled; but a dawn of a new morning is God' grace. If you need a testimony about God's grace, then IF I

SHOULD DIE BEFORE I WAKE will encourage your soul. Nothing happens in our lives by chance. If you need a miracle, God's got that too. Trust Him. Has it been a while since you've had a testimony? Increase your prayer life, build your faith and walk in victory because without a test, there is no testimony.

THE GUILTY
SERIES
KICK OFF

GUILTY OF LOVE

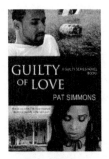

When do you know the most important decision of your life is the right one?

Reaping the seeds from what she's sown; Cheney Reynolds moves into a historic neighborhood in Ferguson, Missouri, and becomes a reclusive. Her first neighbor, the incomparable Mrs. Beatrice Tilley Beacon aka Grandma BB, is an opinionated childless widow. Then there is Parke Kokumuo Jamison VI, a direct descendant of a royal African tribe. He learned his family ancestry, African history, and lineage preservation before he could count. Unwittingly, they are drawn to each other, but it takes Christ to weave their lives into a spiritual bliss while He exonerates their past indiscretions.

—NOT GUILTY OF LOVE—

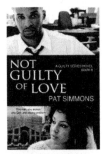

One man, one woman, one God and one big problem. Malcolm Jamieson wasn't the man who got away, but the man God instructed Hallison Dinkins to set free. Instead of their explosive love affair leading them to the wedding altar, God diverted Hallison to the prayer altar.

Malcolm was convinced that his woman had loss her mind to break off their engagement. Didn't Hallison know that Malcolm, a tenth generation descendant of a royal African tribe, couldn't be replaced? Once Malcolm concedes that their relationship can't be savaged, he issues Hallison his own edict, "If we're meant to be with each other, we'll find our way back. If not, that means that there's a love stronger than what we had." Someone has to retreat, and God never loses a battle.

—STILL GUILTY—

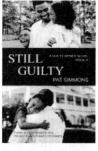

Cheney Reynolds Jamieson made a choice years ago that is now shaping her future and the future of the men she loves. A botched abortion left her unable to carry a baby to term, and her husband, Parke K. Jamison VI, is expected to produce heirs. With a wife who cannot give him a child, Parke vows to find and get custody of his illegitimate son by any means necessary. Meanwhile, Cheney's twin brother, Rainey, struggles with his anger over his ex-girlfriend's actions that haunt him, and their father, Dr. Roland Reynolds, fights to keep an old secret in the past.

THE GUILTY PARTIES SERIES

—THE ACQUITTAL—

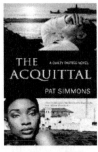

Two worlds apart, but their hearts dance to the same African drum beat. On a professional level, Dr. Rainey Reynolds is a competent, highly sought-after orthodontist. Inwardly, he needs to be set free from the chaos of revelations that make him question if happiness is obtainable. To get away from the drama, Rainey is willing to leave the country under the guise of a mission trip with Dentist Without Borders. Will changing his surroundings really change him? Ghanaian beauty Josephine Abena Yaa Amoah returns to Africa after completing her studies in America. She prays for Rainey's surrender to Christ in order for God to acquit him of his self-inflicted mental torture. In the Motherland of Ghana, Africa, Rainey not only visits the places of his ancestors, will he embrace the liberty that Christ's Blood really does set every man free.

—THE CONFESSION—

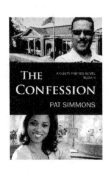

Sandra Nicholson, Kidd and Ace Jamieson's mother is on the threshold of happiness, but Kidd believes no man is good enough for his mother, especially if her love interest could be a man just like his absentee father.

THE JAMIESON LEGACY SERIES

—GUILTY BY ASSOCIATION—

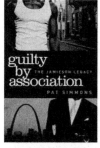

How important is a name? To the St. Louis Jamiesons who are tenth generation descendants of a royal African tribe—everything. To the Boston Jamiesons whose father never married their mother—there is no loyalty or legacy. Kidd Jamieson suffers from the "angry" male syndrome because his father was an absent in the home, but insisted his two sons carry his last name. It takes an old woman who mingles genealogy truths and Bible verses together for Kidd to realize his worth as a strong black man. He learns it's not his association with the name that identifies him, but the man he becomes that defines him.

—THE GUILT TRIP—

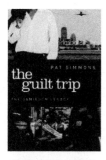

Aaron "Ace" Jamieson is living a carefree life. He's good-looking, respectable when he's in the mood, but his weakness is women. If a woman tries to ambush him with a pregnancy, he takes off in the other direction. It's a lesson learned from his absentee father that responsibility is optional. Talise Rogers has a bright future ahead of her. She's pretty and has no problem catching a man's eye, which is exactly what she does with Ace. Trapping Ace Jamieson is the furthest thing from Taleigh's mind when she learns she pregnant and Ace rejects her. "I want nothing from you Ace, not even your name." And Talise meant it.

—FREE FROM GUILT—

It's salvation round-up time and Cameron Jamieson's name is on God's hit list.

Although his brothers and cousins embraced God—thanks to the women in their lives—the two-degreed MIT graduate isn't going to let any woman take him down that path without a fight. He's satisfied with his career, social calendar, and good genes. But God uses a beautiful messenger, Gabrielle Dupree, to show him that he's in a spiritual deficit. Cameron learns the hard way that man's wisdom is like foolishness to God. For every philosophical argument he throws her way, Gabrielle exposes him to scriptures that makes him question his worldly knowledge.

THE CARMEN SISTERS SERIES

—NO EASY CATCH—

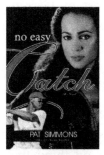

Shae Carmen discovered that her boyfriend was not only married, but on the verge of reconciling with his estranged wife. Humiliated, Shae begins to second guess herself as why she didn't see the signs that he was nothing more than a devil's decoy masquerading as a devout Christian man. St. Louis Outfielder Rahn Maxwell finds himself a victim of an attempted carjacking. The Lord guides him out of harms' way by opening the gunmen's eyes to Rahn's identity and they direct him out of their ambush! When the news media gets wind of what happened with the baseball player, Shae's television station lands an exclusive interview. Just when Shae lets her guard down, she is faced with another scandal that rocks her world. This time the stakes are higher. Not only is her heart on the line, so is her professional credibility.

—IN DEFENSE OF LOVE—

Lately, nothing in Garrett Nash's life has made sense. When two people close to the U.S. Marshal wrong him deeply, Garrett expects God to remove them from his life. Instead, the Lord relocates Garrett to another city to start over, as if he were the offender instead of the victim.

Criminal attorney Shari Carmen is comfortable in her own skin—most of the time. Being a "dark and lovely" African-American sister has its challenges, especially when it comes to relationships. While playing tenor saxophone at an anniversary party, she grabs the attention of Garrett Nash. And as God draws them closer together, He makes another request of Garrett, one to which it will prove far more difficult to say "Yes, Lord."

—REDEEMING HEART—

Landon Thomas brings a new definition to the word "prodigal," as in prodigal son, brother or anything else imaginable. It's a good thing that God's love covers a multitude of sins, but He isn't letting Landon off easy. His journey from riches to rags proves to be humbling and a lesson well learned.

Real Estate Agent Octavia Winston is a woman on a mission, whether it's God's or hers professionally. One thing is for certain, she's not about to compromise when it comes to a Christian mate, so why did God send a homeless man to steal her heart?

Minister Rossi Tolliver (Crowning Glory) knows how to minister to God's lost sheep and through God's redemption, the game changes for Landon and Octavia.

—DRIVEN TO BE LOVED—

On the surface, Brecee Carmen has nothing in common with Adrian Cole. She is a pediatrician certified in trauma care; he is a transportation problem–solver for a luxury car dealership (a.k.a., a car salesman). Neither one of them is sure that they're compatible. To complicate matters, Brecee is the sole unattached Carmen daughter when it seems as though everyone else around her—family and friends—is finding love. Through a series of discoveries, Adrian and Brecee learn that things don't always happen by coincidence. Generational forces are at work, keeping promises, protecting family members, and perhaps even drawing Adrian back to the church he had strayed from. Is it possible that God has been playing matchmaker all along?

SINGLE TITLES

—CROWNING GLORY—

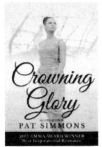

Cinderella had a prince; Karyn Wallace has a King.

While Karyn served four years in prison for an unthinkable crime, she embraced salvation through Crowns for Christ outreach ministry. After her release, Karyn stays strong and confident, despite the stigma society places on ex-offenders. Since Christ strengthens the underdog, Karyn refuses to sway away from the scripture, "He who the Son has set free is free indeed."

Levi Tolliver is steadfast there is a price to pay for every sin committed, especially after the untimely death of his wife during a robbery. Then Karyn enters Levi's life. He is enthralled not only with her beauty, but her sweet spirit until he learns about her incarceration. If Levi can accept that Christ paid Karyn's debt in full, then a treasure awaits him.

—TALK TO ME—

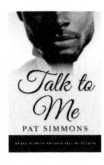

Despite being deaf as a result of a fireworks explosion, CEO of a St. Louis non-profit company, Noel Richardson, expertly navigates the hearing world. What some view as a disability, Noel views as a challenge—his lack of hearing has never held him back.

It also helps that he has great looks, numerous university degrees, and full bank accounts. But those assets don't define him as a man who longs for the right woman in his life.

Deciding to visit a church service, Noel is blind-sided by the most beautiful and graceful Deaf interpreter he's ever seen. Mackenzie Norton challenges him on every level through words and signing, but as their love grows, their faith is tested.

When their church holds a yearly revival, they witness the healing power of God in others. Mackenzie has faith to believe that Noel can also get in on the blessing. Since faith comes by hearing, whose voice does Noel hear in his heart, Mackenzie or God's?

—HER DRESS—

Sometimes a woman just wants to splurge on something new, especially when she's about to attend an event with movers and shakers. Find out what happens when Pepper Trudeau is all dressed up and goes to the ball, but another woman is modeling the same attire. At first, Pepper is embarrassed, then the night gets interesting when she meets Drake Logan. Her Dress is a romantic novella about the all too common occurrence— two women shopping at the same place. Maybe having the same taste isn't all bad. Sometimes a good dress is all you need to meet the man of your dreams.

Check out my fellow Christian fiction authors
writing about faith, family and love
with African-American characters.
You won't be disappointed!

#BlackChristianReads

www.blackchristianreads.com

CPSIA information can be obtained
at www.ICGtesting.com
Printed in the USA
LVOW04s1539280416

485769LV00019B/886/P

9 780692 434406